THE UGLY HUSBAND

by

Joey D'Angelo

First published by Black Champagne 2024

This novel is entirely a work of fiction. The names, characters and incidents portrayed in it are the work of the author's imagination. Any resemblance to actual persons, living or dead, events or localities is entirely coincidental.

First edition

ISBN: 978-0-6454627-3-9

Chapter 1

M y loving wife is in a foul mood.
I can sense it even before the chilly, late-Spring wind blows me through our front door. There is rage radiating from the kitchen, as though a lion is caged back there.

Claire's greeting is a scowl, her acknowledgment of my presence squeezed through clenched teeth. Even the potatoes she's chopping look skittish. I have no idea what to think - have I done something wrong?

"Did something happen today babe?" I ask, hating the timidity of my voice.

"No. Not really." She chews at her jaw and looks into the distance. She's lying.

I drop my keys on the kitchen bench and take off my work jacket. It's hard to keep my voice even-tempered.

"Have *I* done something wrong?"

She considers this, shakes her head. The relief makes my shoulders sag a little.

"Simone came over today."

"Oh. How are her little ones?"

"Steve has been cheating on her." Claire's tone is abruptly venomous.

She chops the potatoes, her knife thudding loudly against the wooden board.

"She found out while they were in Sydney. He's been fucking all these other women, and prostitutes, strippers... she doesn't know how many."

"Oh shit. Really?"

It's hard to imagine; Steve is this weedy guy, glasses, acne scars. Don't get me wrong, I like Steve – he doesn't talk too much, he's into music, he owns his own business - but I never would have considered him some sort of shady Casanova.

"I can't picture it."

"They were at the hotel with the kids and he just went off somewhere by himself. She knew something was up. When he came back, he got straight into the swimming pool and she went through his phone. All these women, all these messages. He was off fucking somebody while Simone and the kids were sitting back at the hotel waiting for him! Fucking bastard!"

I shake my head in disbelief. Who could have known that boring little shit could be so sly. And so horny, apparently.

There must be something in my face because Claire is glaring at me, her cheeks turning bright red.

"Oh you like that, right?" she spits. "That sounds great, does it? Fucking other women, fucking *prostitutes*! You'd love to do that, wouldn't you?"

"What? What the fuck does it have to do with *me*?"

"I can see that you're thinking he's a fucking hero or something, messing around with other women while his wife looks after their children… is that what you're doing too?"

I can't help but laugh.

The very idea is ridiculous. I've barely spoken to another woman in months.

"Yeah you *would* just laugh at me, wouldn't you. *Prick*." Her eyes are bulging.

I realise that she's serious. Against my better judgement, my temper stirs.

I'm *not* cheating on my wife, by the way. I never have and I never would.

I love my family and I work my ass off to keep us afloat. And even if I *wanted* to, I wouldn't have time to fuck anybody else if there was ever a chance of that happening.

Which there isn't. For half my life, I've made a point of avoiding any sort of interaction with other women, even those I'm attracted to.

Especially those I'm attracted to.

She's transferring her anger at Steve on to me. It's bullshit, but I have to tread carefully. The wrong word here could make our home a cold hell for me and our kids.

I don't get a chance to speak anyway.

"I *know* you're not cheating on me. I *know* you're not fucking anyone else. Nobody else would *have* you. Nobody would want be with you. Except *me*."

She spits the last words bitterly.

It feels like I've been punched in the stomach.

Did she *really* just say that?

I'm lost for words.

"No one else would put up with your shit, Joe. Nobody would ever want to fuck *you*. I *know* I don't have to worry about you cheating on me."

I don't know what to say.

She seems satisfied and goes back to preparing dinner.

Chapter 2

T he car door slams shut behind me and before I can even turn around, my family zooms off down the highway.

I watch it until it disappears over the next hill - my revving car, my crying kids, my furious wife, all leaving me abandoned beside the highway in the blazing summer sun.

By the time I realize my phone and wallet are still in the car's console, they're long gone.

I'm stuck.

It probably wouldn't be such a big deal if I hadn't been so sick yesterday. Properly, stinky sick. I spent all morning sweating in my office, until my boss sent me home at lunchtime.

All I had wanted to do today was doze and recuperate. I was supposed to go to a buck's party tonight and I needed to save some energy. I've been looking forward to Ben's buck's night for weeks and I was determined to go, sick or not.

But instead of letting me rest up, Claire dragged me to some Farmer's Market first thing this morning. Despite the fact I was pale and unsteady and clearly sick, she insisted that I come along.

"Spend some time with your family, for god's sake."

"Claire, I'm not well. I was sent home from work yesterday…"

"Yeah so you could mope around by yourself and fall asleep all the time."

"I'm feeling pretty sick babe…"

Her sniff says it all. Men don't get sick. They just get lazy. *Lazier.*

"The girls want to do something with you today." Her arms crossed over her chest. "And so do I. The market won't go all day."

"I'm really not up for it babe…"

"Not up for being a father to your daughters?"

Right.

A couple of hours later I find myself at a Farmer's Market.

The sun is oppressive and hard to escape. I find myself an empty deck chair and crawl into it while she tells one of the stallholders about her grandfather's legendary tomatoes.

It feels like I'm dying. Little K, our youngest daughter, comes over and climbs into my lap. I wonder if she's getting sick too. I take my hat off and balance it on her soft blonde curls, giving her what shade I can. In moments, she's asleep on my chest. I hold her gently, staring up at the sky, trying to block out the noise of the market.

Then I'm rudely nudged awake by a Claire's knee pushing against my shoulder. She and our other daughter, Big M, are standing next to us.

"Wake up! What the hell is wrong with you?" Claire is scowling down at me. "You're going to get sunburnt."

"Oh. Sorry."

"You've been asleep for an *hour,* the market's almost finished."

"Oh. Good."

Her scowl deepens.

"I don't know why you even bothered coming."

I've got no response for that.

"Come on. We're leaving."

Thank Christ.

I shake Little K gently. She groans beneath my hat and tries to stay asleep, her chubby face scarlet and damp from the heat. I feel terrible insisting, but she doesn't cry, just opens her eyes and flops around.

I manage to stand up with her held to my chest, even though my head spins and my stomach churns. Dozing in the sun *was* a terrible idea, to be fair.

Claire stalks back to the car, her hackles clearly showing. I lurch along after her with Little K wriggling against my chest. My daughter flops into her car seat, blinking slowly, and Big M settles in next to her, rolling her eyes.

I climb into the passenger seat with a relieved sigh. The coolness of the car's interior is a blessing, but the comfort doesn't last long.

Claire's eyes are wide, her voice poisonous.

"I can't fucking *believe* you would embarrass me like that!"

"Embarrass you?" I'm sun-dazed and dopey and have no idea what she's talking about. "In front of who?"

"You were *sleeping* in the middle of the market!"

"Did you see somebody we know?"

"That's not the *point* and you know it. I just wanted a nice day out with my family and you can't even fucking do that!"

I can hear the girls squirming in the back seat, so I try to calm their mother down.

"Babe…"

"Don't fucking babe me!"

"Not in front of the girls Claire, come on…"

"Oh you're such a *good* fucking father." She stomps on the accelerator and the car zooms haphazardly out of the parking lot. The girls and I hold on for dear life. "You would be an even better father if you could be bothered *staying awake* when we're trying to do things as a family."

"I've been pretty crook, Claire. I *said* I didn't want to come."

"Of *course* you didn't want to come."

She reefs on the steering wheel and we change lanes, heading out of the city.

I don't want to ask, but I have to.

"Claire… where are we going?"

"Mum's having an afternoon tea." She doesn't look at me. "Everyone's going to be there."

My stomach sinks.

Her mother lives about an hour out of the city. Her family, lacking even the mildest dysfunction, is painfully boring. I can see the afternoon stretching out into pleasantly polite purgatory in a small dining room with no air conditioning.

"Babe." I take a deep breath, trying to settle my gut. "I don't think I'm up to it. I'm still pretty sick. I've just been asleep in the sun for an hour and… Ben's buck's party is tonight, remember?"

"Too bad. You should have thought of that before you went to sleep."

"But it's already two o'clock. The buck's starts at five. I won't make it back in time to get ready."

"Why would you bother going? Do you even *know* the girl he's marrying?"

"Ben asked me to come. In person. We've

9

known each other for nearly ten years babe…"

"But you've never hung out with him, it's not like he's your friend."

She's half right - Ben and I haven't hung out much outside of work, but we get along well. I think we could be buddies if we had the chance. Going to his buck's - especially after being personally invited - would be a solid step in that direction. I don't have that many friends. Claire knows that.

The sudden swirl of butterflies in my stomach makes me feel even sicker.

"I feel like I'm dying. Can you please just drop me at home?"

"We don't have time."

"It's not a uni exam. It's lunch at your mums. I'm sure they'll forgive you for being ten minutes late."

"It's afternoon tea and you're coming with us." Claire's eyes never leave the highway. "We can at least pretend to be a family for a couple of hours."

A familiar ache tweaks in my chest.

"Fine. Whatever. I'll just do what I'm fucking told, as usual…"

The brakes squeal and the car lurches. Suddenly we're veering across two lanes of traffic to get to the breakdown lane. Claire stomps on the brakes and we all bounce in our seats.

Her eyes are wide, wild.

Fuck.

"*Get out then!*"

She doesn't moderate her voice. It's a full, furious scream that sets both girls off crying.

"*Go on!* Get out of the fucking car you can *fucking walk home!*"

With her voice tearing through my fuddled head, I open the car door and stumble out onto the side of the highway. Her words follow me out, the screech of a relentless hawk.

"You fucking *bastard*! Don't be at home when we get back then! Just *fuck off!*"

The car door slams.

Off they go, leaving me sick in the sun on the side of the highway.

So I walk. No money, no phone, no choice.

The heat feels deadly.

Home is about 12km away, all uphill. I reckon it'll take about three hours. If I was fit and it was night time, I would dance it in, no problem.

But I feel like a zombie. And it's the middle of a summer afternoon. Cars are zooming past in all their air-conditioned glory. The soles of my shoes are already warming up.

I can do this.

Walking gives me time to think.

11

Chapter 3

It hasn't always been this way between Claire and I. Once, we were young and insanely in love. I haven't forgotten, but I often wonder if *she* has.

We first got together when we were both nineteen. It's corny, but I can still remember the first time I saw her; walking through the UTAS campus in Mowbray, textbooks clutched to her chest, bottle-blond hair flapping around her shoulders as she laughed with her friend.

I saw her and I knew - this was the girl I wanted to grow up with. And grow up we did.

Heady times. Both of us were explorers on the frontiers of our sexuality; I had spent the previous summer hooking up with as many girls as I could, and she was getting a reputation as somebody who liked making out with random dudes at parties.

When we first got together, I remember being somewhat surprised that she was a virgin. She told me there had been a couple of false starts, but it just hadn't worked out for one reason or another.

So we didn't have sex straight away. We waited. I didn't mind.

There was something about her that I was deeply drawn to. Unlike the other girls I was attracted to, I didn't fantasize about her. She was too pure to be leched upon by my degenerate visions.

Don't get me wrong, I wanted to be inside her more and more each day but… I just couldn't visualise it.

She was too perfect. She existed in some higher-plane, far beyond the sweaty realms of teenage sex. She was magical, spiritual, and I couldn't imagine myself desecrating her temple.

That changed eventually, of course.

There was a café she liked to visit, not far from campus, and we started meeting there for lunch every now and then. It was mid-Autumn and we would always order the same thing; she would get a chicken noodle soup and I would get a large cappuccino.

The café offered several tables outside in the sunshine, but as the weather turned cold we spent more time inside, where the padded booths offered warmth, comfort and privacy.

We had been together for about a month by this stage, and it was increasingly hard to keep our hands off each other. There was a booth towards the back of the café where we could chat and make out without interruption.

The café's owner, an Italian man in his late forties, would grin and raise his eyebrows as we made ourselves at home, but if he was offended or upset by our constant snogging, he never made it known.

We were largely out of sight of the rest of the customers and after a while, that booth started to feel like home.

One afternoon, after our cups were emptied, we were hugging and kissing when things suddenly went to the next level; her hand had drifted down to the front of my jeans, where an embarrassing bulge was throbbing just below my zipper.

I gasped into her mouth. We had felt each other up once or twice in the heat of the moment, but this was the first time she had touched me so blatantly, with such purpose.

She smiled as I squirmed, with a hungry look in her eyes that I came to know very well in the years that followed. Her hand didn't move away; in fact it squeezed, massaging my stiffness through my jeans, exploring my hardness, making me gasp again.

She giggled and looked around; we had the café more or less to ourselves. There were a few people sitting at the tables outside and the Italian was nowhere to be seen. When she looked back at me, she was biting her lip.

"I don't think I had enough to eat," she told me in a quiet, husky voice.

"What?" I was stupefied with horniness. She laughed again at the expression on my face.

"I'm *hungry*," she whispered and leaned in closer. "I want to *taste* you."

Lost for words, I could only let her push me back in the booth's padded seat. Her cheeks were flushed and lovely, and as we kissed again I felt her small fingers pull down my zipper.

"What are you... *oh...*"

For a moment I was washed with relief as the pressure in my cock was eased by the loosening of my jeans – but moments later electricity pulsed throughout my entire body as her hands returned to work.

With another quick glance around the café, she pulled my hard cock out of my jeans. My breath was coming in short, sharp gasps as she tickled along my shaft, gently stroking me with her fingertips. She shuffled back in her seat, leaning over my lap, and I heard her murmur softly, almost to herself.

"Oh, it's *beautiful.*"

Her warm breath made the head of my cock

tingle, but before I could say anything I felt her tongue slowly licking its way up my shaft. Her tongue was wet and warm and soft but rough, a kitten's tongue.

My entire body shuddered; it felt *so* good.

She licked it again with a hungry sigh. I was transfixed by the sight of her delicate pink tongue dragging over the taut skin of my cock.

When she opened her soft lips wider and took my hardness into her mouth, it took an effort not to moan out loud. Her warmth enveloped my stiffness and she pushed down, taking my cock further and further.

My hands grabbed the back of the booth's padded seat and I looked around the café, my cheeks burning. Nobody was paying us any attention, so I relaxed a little and pushed my hips towards her bobbing face.

She moaned, her mouth full of my cock, and I felt her tongue beating against my shaft. Her lips were tight around me and she sucked hungrily, making me squirm. I had to bite my lips as she took me deeper, and I could feel the pressure building, feel my cock swelling against the soft wetness of her throat.

"Stop!" I gasped, trying to keep my voice down. "I'm gonna… gonna…"

She didn't stop. In fact, her head bobbed faster

and faster and she sucked even harder as I closed my eyes and tried to stifle another moan.

I could feel the orgasm building throughout my entire body, my nerves thrummed and my mind was blank.

Even with my eyes squeezed shut, I felt her soft hand close around the base of my cock and squeeze. Her delicious mouth was relentless, sucking and licking even as the cum pulsed out of me and into her throat.

My entire body shook in the most intense orgasm I had ever known.

I felt my seed pumping into her mouth over and over and she sucked it down greedily, drawing out every last drop.

My feet thrummed against the floor.

I forgot where I was. I forgot *who* I was.

I gasped and whimpered, shuddered again and again as she licked at the head of my cock, cleaning up every last pearl of cum.

It took an effort to open my eyes again and I stroked the back of her neck, my body awash with sparkling warmth.

The café was still empty – but as I looked up, I saw the kitchen door swinging lightly on its hinges.

Had somebody just passed by? It didn't matter and I forgot about it, trying to catch my breath.

A few moments later she, pushed my softening dick back into my jeans and pulled up my zipper.

When she sat back up, her cheeks were flushed a gorgeous shade of pink, and her lips were shining. She was beaming, pleased with herself, her eyes half-lidded.

I kissed her on the cheek and let out a long sigh of satisfaction that made her laugh.

We thought we were so naughty, and she giggled fitfully as we went up to the small counter and paid for our coffee.

She didn't notice the Italian's appreciative smile, but I sure did and my cheeks flushed with embarrassment.

Not that it mattered; the Italian barely looked at me. His attention was fully on Claire and I could see the desire in his eyes, even as I put an arm around her and led her away.

"See you soon," he called as we walked out of his café. "Make sure you come again!"

We both burst out laughing.

Chapter 4

W e moved in together as soon as we could and we married in our early twenties - not because she was pregnant, not because our parents thought it was for the best, not because we wanted a new blender.

We married because we were *crazy* about each other, and that was that.

We were inseparable. We spent our twenties partying, working, and setting our lives up for the long term. Even our friends told us that our enduring relationship was something special, something they looked up to.

Nobody else would have you.

Big M was born after we had been married for seven years and Little K arrived soon afterwards. For a while, we existed in a bubble of familiar bliss.

Claire stopped partying, I partied far less. We lost contact with some of our party animal friends - some of whom were amongst our oldest friends -

but it just felt like we were trimming the fat.

When Little K was around three years old, Claire started going out again. We never had anybody to babysit for us, so the idea was that we would take turns going out.

We didn't take turns.

Claire had some catching up to do.

Even though I more or less stopped going out as well when Big M was born, Claire felt that I had been living it up. To hear her tell it, I had been a rollicking drunk, partying the weekends away while she shouldered all the work of raising a baby, then a toddler, then another baby.

It wasn't true. I've gone out maybe a dozen times over the last five years. Probably less.

But I didn't mind too much. I was smoking more and more weed so I wasn't too interested in going out anyway. There were PlayStation games to play, mountains of corn chips and plenty of beer.

My family was safe and sound and fed and warm and that was enough for me.

I was happy to see her partying with her friends and enjoying herself. Sometimes when she got home, tipsy and full of beans, I would get laid.

Most of the time, life seemed pretty good.

Chapter 5

I t's getting harder and harder to lift my feet, to keep walking. The sun is wearing me down.

I've made it to Cornelian Bay, a huge picnic area not far from the river, so I stop at a park bench in the shade. Luckily, my tobacco pouch is in my pocket so I pull it out and roll up a small joint.

Another bad idea. I'm only halfway through smoking it when my head starts spinning. My body is weak in the sun, like dry tissue paper, but I take another drag.

I wonder how afternoon tea is going. wonder how Claire explained my absence to my doubtlessly sympathetic in-laws.

My stomach heaves.

Suddenly I'm on my feet, running towards the nearest rubbish bin, vomiting into the stink of old barbeque leftovers and empty orange juice bottles.

When I'm done, it takes a real effort to stand up straight. The sun is dizzying. I hold on to the sides of the bin to steady myself. My head is clouded, stoned, exhausted. My thumb glides into some kind of unidentifiable sludge.

There is a family at one of the barbeques just a stone throw away. All of them are staring at me in disgust - mum paused with a bowl of salad in her hands, kids covering their mouths and scrunching up their noses, dad glaring at me from the barby.

I throw up again, squeezing my eyes closed against the shame of it all, keeping them closed until I hear an angry voice.

"What the *fuck?*"

The Dad has thrown his barbeque tongs onto the picnic table and he's marching towards me. Mum calls after him - "Harry, don't!" - but he ignores her.

I bolt. Well, I try to. My legs are jelly. I shamble over the grass, making a beeline away from the family barbeque.

I manage to resist looking over my shoulder until I reach the footpath. Dad is standing on the grass, watching me go, hands on his hips, a scowl on his face. I cross the road, quickly, and he stops watching me and walks back to his family, his shoulders back, his head held high.

I throw the joint in the gutter and keep walking.

It's almost dark by the time I get home. Claire and the girls still aren't back from her mother's, which is a blessed relief.

I'm exhausted. I'm dirty. And I stink, by god do I stink.

Nobody would ever want to fuck you.

It's understandable, I guess.

I go outside and smoke a joint in my underwear. It doesn't make me throw up this time.

The muffling blanket it spreads across my thoughts is a welcome relief. The aching in my feet subsides to a dull roar. I smoke the joint slowly, willing it to calm the churning in my gut as well. It helps a little.

I limp into the shower, scrub and dry, then collapse into bed.

It's almost nine o'clock. The buck's party would be well and truly raging by now.

I don't even care anymore.

I just need to sleep.

Chapter 6

L ast to bed, first to rise. It's a new week.
My morning routine doesn't change much;
glass of water, piss, get breakfast for the girls,
make a coffee and read my phone while I wait
for everyone else to stumble out of bed.

The girls get up next, crabby and hungry, their
hair twisted into weird shapes. Their bickering
usually summons Claire soon afterwards.

I quickly get dressed while they have breakfast
and take turns showering. I'll get the girls dressed
for school while Claire chooses and discards half
a dozen outfits for the day. While she makes up
her mind, I'm out the door to catch my bus.

I leave at *exactly* the same time, every day – if
I miss my bus, the next one doesn't come for an
hour.

This morning, she gets up late and comes out
scowling, her phone clutched to her chest. She
barks at the girls to stop arguing about which cup

is bigger (the cups are identical) and they do.

Unless things speed up a bit, I'll have to leave while Big M is in the shower. I try and hurry the girls along with their breakfast, to a chorus of complaints.

"Just let them eat," Claire growls. "I can't listen to it this morning."

She stalks off to the kitchen and I hear a loud bang.

"Babe?" I call. "You okay?"

No answer, just another bang, a drawer being slammed closed. I stick my head into the kitchen.

"Claire?"

"There's no fucking coffee." Her eyes are furious, her hair wild.

"Yeah. I left you half of what was there but…"

"You might as well have had it all." Her hands move sharply, angrily, shoving things pointlessly around the kitchen bench. "Or you could have just not had one."

"Sorry. I'll get more tonight."

She shrugs, her lips twisted, so I leave her to it. A series of bangs and cracks follows me down the hallway as she takes her temper out on the crockery.

"Come on girls, eat up, it's almost time for a shower."

Both girls protest; they don't want a shower.

Claire stomps into the room and sits down at the table with a steaming cup of black tea and a slice of toast. At this rate the girls will be late for school and Claire will be late for work. I've only got about five minutes before I need to leave for the bus stop.

"You need a shower," I try to reason with the midgets. "You can't go to school without…"

"Just leave it." Claire orders me sharply.

"Oh. Okay."

She frowns at me. "Why are you so fucking anxious? What's your problem?"

It catches me off guard. I put my hands up defensively.

"I'm fine, babe. Well… I *was* fine until about five seconds ago…"

She slams her cup on the wooden table and glares at me.

"You know, it's not always just about you, Joe. I'm having a *crap* morning and the least you could do is give a shit."

"Sorry, I'm just trying to get everyone moving so you're not late."

"Whatever." She turns away from me, dismissive, and gazes out the window.

Nobody would ever want you.

"Right. I've gotta go."

I kiss the girls goodbye.

I lean in to kiss Claire's cheek and she stiffens, barely tolerating it.

"You're just going to leave me to get the girls ready. Great."

Anger radiates from her.

"Babe, I can't miss my bus."

"Fine, whatever, just go." She turns back to the window.

For a moment I'm frozen to the spot, unsure of what to say or do, then I shake my head and head for the front door.

"*Selfish bastard,*" she mutters, loudly enough for me to hear.

As I open the front door, I hear Little K ask her mother what a bastard is.

I'm out the door and gone before I can hear the answer.

Chapter 7

I t's a bit after midnight. I'm at home, the kids are in bed.

Claire is out clubbing with her friends.

I'm bored, depressed, wasting time on the computer reading about White Ribbon Day.

A *Facebook* notification appears in my browser window, a private message from… Ronnie?

The only Ronnie I've ever known was a kid in my Grade Two class who moved to Melbourne before I got to know him. There is no profile pic, just a grey shape. It must be spam.

I'm bored enough to click over to it anyway.

Ronnie: So nice to meet you gorgeous! Omg you're such a good dancer!

Wow, maybe it's not spam, maybe just a wrong…

Ronnie: You didn't leave did you? I want another kiss xxx

That's brilliant. I'm about to bag this guy out for being given a dud name by whichever woman he was hitting on, when I realise...

Facebook isn't logged in to my account.

It's logged in to Claire's.

I'm seeing messages meant for my wife.

I'm still reeling when another message appears
– from Claire. She must be responding from her
phone.

Claire: I'm still here, cum and find me x

Oh.

My world is suddenly very, very fragile.

My breath won't come.

My heart is pounding.

A photo appears. It's Claire. A bathroom selfie
from whichever club she's at.

She's bent over her phone, her lids lowered, lips
pursed, shoulders hunched.

She looks *good*.

Then another selfie. This one with a deliberate
hint of cleavage.

My stomach is turning to ice.

Ronnie: Such a fucking spunk

Claire: Lol yes I am! Hurry up xxx

Ronnie: Naughty girl lol... I'm on my way x

I stare at the computer for another hour, wavering between fury and sickness.

They don't message each other again.

Chapter 8

I 'm in a daze. My gut churns constantly.

The world floats past. I don't see it or hear it. I certainly don't take part.

At work I stare at my monitor for hours. There's not much to do. If there was, I wouldn't do it. I barely speak to anyone and after a couple of hours my workmates stay well clear of me.

Claire didn't get home until well after 3am. I pretended to be asleep.

My wife is cheating on me.

I don't know what to say. I don't know what to do.

I never thought that Claire would find somebody else.

Our relationship, the backbone of my life, is crumbling.

Should I confront her? Should I scream and cry and beg and tear my clothes and get on my knees and ask her *why?*

Why I'm not enough.

Why our *family* isn't enough.

Why she had to go and fuck around.

Why why why.

There's nobody I can talk to. Nobody that I trust.

I can't see a way out.

I can't leave her. I can't leave my family, my home. My daughters.

I don't want to go home, but I've got nowhere else to go.

Nobody else would have you.

I think about dying.

I think about running away.

I think about dying some more.

I call my superannuation company to find out how much of a payout my family would get if I died suddenly. In a car accident, for instance.

Not much. Not enough, not nearly enough.

Chapter 9

This morning it's raining - heavy, sweet-smelling summer rain.

I'm waiting at the bus stop in my heavy jacket.

I watch a girl walk down the hill past our house. I've never seen her before. She's wearing a clean white hoodie, blue jeans and a loose scarf.

She reaches the bus stop and smiles at me in the rain. She has light auburn hair and her smile is refreshingly unaffected.

"Good morning."

"Good morning," I do my best to smile. The bus is coming down the hill, so I say "You've got great timing…"

She smiles at me, blank, tilting her head.

"The bus is here," I tell her gently, nodding toward, the bus. She follows my gaze through the haze.

"Oh, yeah. Cool."

The bus pulls up next to us. As one, the girl and

I both step back and gesture at the bus door.

"You first…"

"After you…"

For a moment we just look at each other, then we both laugh.

It feels good to laugh. Really, really good.

"You first," she insists. "You've been waiting in the rain for longer."

Arguing would make it awkward, so I smile at her again and step onto the bus. The bus driver is chuckling at us.

I take my usual seat at the back of the bus.

She takes the very first seat, right at the front… but she glances up at me as she sits down, that sweet smile still playing on her lips.

When she steps off the bus, there seems to be a spring in her step. Maybe I imagined it, but I watch her go, marvelling at the sunshine that's blooming in my chest. It's a feeling I haven't had for a long, long time.

It feels fantastic.

Chapter 10

I 've decided not to kill myself.

I've thought about it a fair bit in the last week or so. In fact, I haven't thought about much else.

But the girls. My girls.

My daughters would grow up with nothing but fading memories of me if I bailed out now.

I can't bear the thought of it.

My girls mean more to me than anything else. There's no reason why any of this should affect their lives – in fact, they don't need to be in any way associated with this bullshit. It's not about the girls. I love them with everything I am, and that's that.

And anyway, I always believed that suicide was intrinsically wrong, a coward's mistake. The ultimate failure of self. Not something that a person like me would ever seriously consider.

But then... Claire changed the sort of person I am. Writing that down for the first time really brings it home. That's what this is really about; the love of my life changed me into a new person.

A person that she apparently cheats on.

A person that I can't stand.

Self-loathing settles over me each morning when I wake up. It's still there when I lay back down to sleep at the end of the day. It's not a new thing; it's a tumour that has been growing, steadily, silently, over many years, eating me away.

I want to live. For now, anyway.

But I can't leave her.

Our lives are inextricably intertwined, my dear Yorrick.

We've been living together for over fifteen years. We have two children, a mortgage we can barely afford, a car we can barely afford, a fuck-tonne of debt that we can't afford. I've watched friends go through divorces; it can ruin the best people.

If I were to leave Claire I would lose my kids and my home. I would be in debt for years to come. Anything I earned would flow directly to her, much as it does now – except that I wouldn't get any of the benefits, like seeing my kids every day or having a comfortable roof over my head. I would probably end up in a share house.

I would be stuck indefinitely, unable to improve my lot, unwilling to leave my kids.

And she wouldn't be single for long.

She probably wouldn't be single at all.

The thought of my girls living with this fucking Ronnie, or any other man, any other father-figure, makes me see red. Nobody will put distance between my daughters and I. Nobody.

So I'll stay. I'll play my part, though perhaps not the part she's expecting me to play.

When the girl on the bus had smiled at me a few days before, it had sent a warm flush throughout my entire a body, a feeling that reminded me what it was like to really feel *alive*.

I'm not going to confront Claire. I'm not going to beg her to stay with me.

I can fix all of this, I know I can.

I'm nobody's stooge, nobody's cuckold. Once upon a time, I was a catch.

If she's putting herself out there, acting like she's single, hooking up with strangers… then maybe I can too.

Nobody else would be with you.

I'm going to change that.

I have no idea how.

But I will.

Chapter 11

It's late.

Claire's asleep in our cold bed. I've been avoiding her.

Not that she's noticed. She's been more cheerful than I've seen her in months, singing with the girls, bouncing on her fucking toes.

I'm a zombie. It's after midnight and I'm writing this, smoking weed, pondering.

There have always been other blokes sniffing around, the whole time Claire and I have been together. I've threatened them, manipulated them, shut them down. In one case, I got a guy fired from his job when he wouldn't stop calling.

She says she doesn't encourage them, and I have no choice but to believe her. I'm probably fooling myself.

As far as I know, she's never been with anybody other than this Ronnie bastard... but what the fuck would I know?

The laptop is still logged into her *Facebook* account. I refresh it every fifteen minutes, but he hasn't messaged her again. I've read through their conversation a dozen times, and each time I just feel worse.

If I'm going to keep on living – and I am - then things need to change.

I can't go on like this.

I need to work out who I am. What I want. What I need. And… where it all went wrong.

When did I become this person that was so easy to cheat on?

Growing up, I had spent far more time around women than men and it seemed to me that the secret to a wonderful life was to keep the women around you happy.

I spent my younger years reading everything I could get my hands on that I thought would help accomplish that; *Cosmo*, *Dolly*, even the *Encyclopaedia of Sex* that I found hidden away at my aunt's house one summer.

All of them were teaching me the skills I thought I needed, namely how to understand, relate to and – most importantly - pleasure women. I hardly thought about anything else.

But I didn't understand the softly spoken language of real seduction. Subtlety passed me by completely.

When I think back now to moments that seemed odd or awkward when I was a teenager, I can see what was really happening - the shy smiles and beckoning nods, the invitations to study, the unexpectedly familiar hand on my shoulder.

I didn't understand discretion. I didn't understand sex as fun, playful, something not to be taken too seriously. I wanted to please, to perform, to be passionate. I wanted it to be meaningful.

I wanted to be swept away by love. I wanted sex to be *special*, meaningful, not rushed, not casual.

I didn't understand why girls who had seemed so friendly would become cold and distant after a while.

I didn't know shit.

But, worse than that, I didn't *know* that I didn't know shit.

I thought I walked the walk.

I was wrong.

Chapter 12

A couple of months before I met Claire, I almost had a threesome.

At the time I was so naïve that I didn't really know what was going on - it was only about ten years later that I realised what I had passed up that night, how rare moments like that would be in a lifetime.

At that age, my mates and I went wherever the party was - which, roughly translated, meant wherever girls were drinking.

A week or two earlier we had met a girl, Bronte, who had her own flat at the top end of Wellington Street even though she was only eighteen. It was a shitty situation; Bronte had been expelled from her school halfway through Grade Twelve and her parents responded by kicking her out of home.

I liked Bronte - I wasn't attracted to her, but I sure respected her. She was tough and far more mature than her years allowed for - she paid her own bills and had a job at a pizza place. Her friends told us that Bronte had her shit together, way more so than her junkie parents.

Even so, her flat quickly became a den of cheap alcohol and precious weed, frequented by an odd mix of her still-in-high-school friends, her brother's stoner mates and random party vultures like me.

So we had been at Bronte's place for a couple of nights in a row, drinking, smoking, playing cards. It was a nice vibe. Even when things started to get messy later in the night it had been fun. Her friends were laid-back, chilled. Most of them were from Prospect, on the opposite side of Launceston from where I grew up, which made them new faces.

There was one face in particular that I was very interested in.

Carmen was unlike any of the other girls I knew. She was tall, full-bodied and exceptionally, startlingly pretty. Her tight jeans showed off a mind-bending figure and her jet-black Merino jumper stretched across firm, insistent breasts.

She clearly came from money - her clothes were new, her long chestnut hair was clean and straight and her earrings glittered brightly in the grimy flat - but here she was, sitting on the same patchy couch, drinking the same cheap wine, smoking the same stanky bong.

Carmen's BFF, Maggie, was her opposite in almost every way.

Maggie was pointy and mean. She wore standard bogan-grunge; skinny black jeans, a faded *Nevermind* skivvy and a blue flannelette shirt several sizes too big for her formlessly skinny frame. Her long hair was lank and bodiless. Her pale, freckled face wore a sneer by default. Her bitter sarcasm was a natural counterpoint to Carmen's languorous, husky laughter.

The two were inseparable though. Maggie barely spoke to anyone other than Carmen, who in turn was fiercely protective of her.

After the first night we all hung out together, Bronte laughingly told me that Carmen was keen on me. It was delightful news - I was very keen on Carmen too. Who wouldn't be?

So by the third time we hung out, we couldn't keep our hands off each other. I expected the stoner dudes to be shitty about it, but to my surprise they all just laughed and teased Carmen about her parents finding out. I remember thinking that her parents must be very strict.

At one point, we were making out so enthusiastically that Bronte kicked us out of the flat. So we went out on to the back steps, in to the cold night air. We didn't mind.

I can still see the half-smile playing across those full lips as she leaned in to kiss me. The wool of her jumper was maddeningly soft. She pulled me close in a way that no girl ever had before - she knew her way around a boy's body.

Before long, my hands were moving beneath her clothes, tickling the small of her back, stroking her taut belly, tracing across her magnificent breasts. I undid her bra with one hand (a trick I learned from Fonzie as a kid) and she pulled it from beneath her jumper, giggling. I kissed her deeply.

When my hand finally cupped the skin of her breast she let out a little moan that made my blood pound. I pulled her jumper up and pushed her nipple towards my lips. Her head rolled back and she clutched at my hair as my tongue worked. I was blown away by the shape of her body.

My hand drifted down her bare back, to the edge of her panties.

She pulled away from me a little, smiling. Her graceful hand drifted down my chest, slowly, until it reached the clasp on my jeans.

My knees started to feel weak.

Biting her lip, she looked me in the eyes as her fingers lightly traced my hard-on through my clothes. I gasped and she grinned.

My thoughts turned scarlet, and I tried to pull her closer… but she stepped away, out of my arms, and composed herself. My body's sense of loss was palpable.

I gaped at her hungrily. She laughed and took my hand.

"Come on," she said. "Let's go inside."

All I could do was follow her back into the flat.

There weren't too many people left – my mate had bailed, leaving only three or four stoners, Maggie, and of course Bronte.

Bronte and Maggie giggled as we came back in. I was flustered and bothered while Carmen was as cool as a mojito.

She led me to an old op-shop arm chair in the corner of the flat, pushed me into it, then sat on the floor facing away from me, leaning back between my knees. I was still hard and trying to hide my dismay.

While one of the stoners was holding court, Carmen waved Maggie over.

The rat-faced girl smirked at me knowingly as she sat next to Carmen on the floor. The two girls put their heads together, whispering and giggling, glancing up at me, gigging again. Eventually Carmen shifted around to face me, laying her cheek on the top of my thigh while her hand stroked the inside of my leg.

Her eyes were bright. I gently pushed her hair behind her ear, trying to ignore her friend.

Carmen bit her lip, grinning up at me.

"I want to see your dick."

I'm pretty sure my mouth dropped wide open.

Maggie snorted laughter, blushing.

Carmen sat up straight and nodded to the doorway that led to the flat's single bedroom.

"We can go in there. Will you let me put it in my mouth?"

I was speechless, breathless. It was the dirtiest thing a girl had ever said to me.

I managed an eager nod and Carmen giggled and raised her eyebrows at Maggie.

Maggie returned the smile, so Carmen ran her hand up my leg again.

"And Maggie too? She wants to suck it as well."

Maggie was blushing, but she still reached out and put her hand on my other thigh, watching my face for a reaction. Carmen was grinning like the cat who got the cream.

"Is that ok? Two girls sucking your big dick?"

Maggie giggled nervously, but she didn't take her hand away. I looked around the room, suddenly fuddled. She had never done anything but scowl at me. Nobody was paying any attention to us.

I didn't want to show Maggie my dick. Not even a little bit.

I definitely didn't want her to touch it.

God, I was so young.

Carmen squeezed my leg. "You'll like it. I promise."

"*Promise…*" echoed Maggie, still blushing. She moved her hand higher up my thigh. A quivering smile was trying to spread across her ratty lips.

Carmen beamed at her friend and wet her lips.

They were waiting for me to say something.

"Um."

Carmen was running her hands over me again, but my hard-on is gone. A look of annoyance flashed over her face so quickly that I might have imagined it.

"You don't want to put it in my mouth?" She feigned sadness, pushing her breasts against my leg.

"I want to put it in your mouth…"

It was so fucking true.

I didn't look at Maggie.

Carmen's smile was slipping.

"I want to taste you. We *both* want to taste you."

Her fingers were gliding up and down my zipper.

My eyes darted to Maggie, then back to Carmen.

"But I've only got one dick," I offered lamely.

Maggie took her hand away.

Disbelief was creeping into Carmen's eyes. With a smile that now seemed forced, she leaned over and whispered into my ear.

"Don't be shy, you'll love it. Maggie gives amazing head."

Despite the churning in my stomach, I held her chin in my fingertips and kissed her slowly.

Maggie was watching.

I tried to whisper.

"I just want you."

Carmen smiled, pleased, but then she leaned in again.

"Go on. Let us play with you. You can even cum in her mouth, if you want to."

I managed not to grimace, but my head was shaking from side to side. When did it start doing that?

Carmen backed off, abruptly, her smile replaced with incredulity.

She looked at Maggie, who snorted and shrugged, then back at me.

That pretty face that I liked so much was now a scornful mask.

Maggie stood up and walked out of the room. Carmen stood as well.

I grabbed her hand.

"Wait! Let's go in there…."

I nodded towards the bedroom door.

She pulled her hand away.

"Wow. Talk about blowing your chances."

She laughed lightly and followed her friend.

Bronte moved out of the flat a week or two later, after some of her stoner friends broke into a neighbouring flat.

I used to see Carmen and Maggie around town - Launceston was, and is, a small place. They would smirk and laugh, rolling their eyes at each other.

It was pretty obvious they didn't want to know me, but once I went over and said hi to Carmen anyway. She was so fucking gorgeous.

She didn't reply. She looked me up and down, as though I were some kind of giant bug, then walked away.

Maggie laughed nastily, trotting along behind her.

Chapter 13

D espite my disappointment, I learned something that night that I would never forget: some girls were just as interested in sex as I was.

Furthermore, some of them were interested in having it with *me*.

If a gorgeous girl like Carmen was willing to share me with her friend, then I must be doing something right.

My confidence soared.

For the next couple of months, I took that confidence and put it to work. I felt like a teenage rock star. Sure, there was angst, embarrassment, depression – all the usual hallmarks of a lower-middle class suburban teenagehood – but I got laid a few times, got my heart broken, tasted that passion I craved so much.

Looking back now at the girls, the parties, the freedom to come and go, the lack of responsibility and the endless horizon… you can tell an eighteen-year-old that they're living the best years of their life, but they'll never believe you.

I was happy. I thought life would always be that way.

Clearly, I didn't know shit.

I fell in love with Claire when I was nineteen and I haven't been with anybody else since.

I loved her with my entire existence. I loved her easy playfulness, her creativity, her dignity, her empathy. I even loved her jealousy.

Her dangerous, wildfire jealousy.

I learned very early on in our relationship to blank any woman who showed interest in me. To break the eye contact, to disengage when the smiles got too friendly.

I learned that lesson far too well – if a woman smiled at me on the street, I looked away. If a woman talked to me at a party, I walked away. If a woman hit on me at a bar, I fucking ran.

They weren't opportunities I was missing – they were bullets I was dodging. I learned that it was easier to avoid flirting all together than it was to extricate yourself from it later on without upsetting anyone.

I was Claire's, and hers alone.

I was happy with that.

I built my life around that.

And now, fifteen years later - I can barely make

eye contact with an attractive woman.

I don't live in a vacuum, of course. You meet people. That's life.

But mostly it was easy to turn cold and disengage with a woman who was showing too much interest in me.

And *that's* what I regret.

Now when I lay awake at night, sleeplessly reflecting on the pivotal moments of my adult life, mourning the times I almost touched the moon, my mind eventually touches on the relationships I didn't have.

It's better to regret something you did, than something you didn't do. The Butthole Surfers said that and it's true.

I've done some shitty stuff in my time - most people have, I hope - but it's the things I didn't do, the things I walked away from, that come back to haunt me the most.

The excitement of a new partner, the thrill of a random one-night stand, the lazy comfort of the stoner fuck buddies I might have had. I've pined for all of those things at one time or another over the last fifteen years and had plenty of opportunities to make good on them.

It's all too easy to replay those scenes in my head - Emily's hand on my thigh as we share a cab home from a work party, Chantelle watching me while she licks a melting ice cream, Joanne's invitation to share a cigarette away from the party ("But I don't smoke…" - what a fucking *dolt*).

Nobody else would want to be with you. Nobody would ever want to fuck you.

For the first time in many, many years, I don't give a fuck what Claire thinks. About anything.

I've pulled away from her, disengaged emotionally, bought out.

You can't have a relationship with somebody who doesn't care about you and she has shown me, again and again, that she doesn't care.

It's not a relationship. It has defaulted into nothing.

I'm not going to try and win her back. It's not my place to.

I won't reach for her. I won't try and seduce her. I won't beg her to be faithful. She's already looking elsewhere, why the hell would I bother?

The first thing I need is some goddamned self-respect. I've been at this woman's beck and call for half my life, and it wasn't enough for her. It's not enough for me anymore either.

If my wife wants me, she can fucking well *show* me she wants me.

And until she does… maybe somebody else will appreciate what I've got to offer.

Somehow, the thought makes me feel better.

I was somebody else once. I was my own person.

I was a man that some woman out there would be happy to have. I was in charge of my own destiny, I had people around me who made me feel good about myself, I had confidence, I had charisma, I had the world at my feet.

I was a man that some woman out there might be interested in fucking.

Could I be that person again?

I think so.

But how?

When I'm not at work, I'm at home. I have gone for months and months without ever speaking to a woman who isn't Claire, my mother, my workmates or a fucking bus driver. Seriously.

And right now, late on this shitty Saturday night, I'm craving something; a conversation with a woman who has no expectations or preconceptions of me.

Somebody who doesn't know me, or Claire, or our lives.

A stranger who is simply happy to talk to me as a man who might be worth talking to.

Somebody I can flirt with.

I go online.

Chapter 14

F*acebook* is not an option – most of my female friends on there are Claire's friends and...

And I want to stay logged into Claire's account. I want to know what my wife is doing. Judge me as you please.

I don't bother with *Ashley Maddison,* an 'affairs' site that was hacked recently, with all their member's data leaked.

I look at *Tinder*, but I keep seeing people that I recognise so I delete it again.

I spend a little while on *Chatroulette*, which I remember seeing at a party a few years ago. The majority of random video feeds feature men pulling their dicks. That gets old very quickly.

It's late by the time I get to *X*, which seems to have a bit more going for it. I've used *X* before, but I've never thought about it as a means to hook up.

I'm pleasantly surprised.

There seems to be a massive community of horny folks using the social media site, posting filthy tweets to each other, sharing porn .gifs, organising swinger parties. A lot of women posting explicit selfies, some anonymously, others with their face or name clearly visible.

There's nothing new about porn on the internet, but this feels different; people are posting pics of themselves, engaging in filthy conversations with strangers, and talking about their lives as well as their desires.

It feels far more real than a passively consumed video or photo on *PornHub*; there are real people behind the booties, people you could actually talk to.

People you might actually meet.

I make an account with a username that reflects how I'm feeling.

TheUglyHusband.

After some mucking around, I learn that you can search for users that are nearby. And not only that, you can search for users nearby who have used a particular keyword in their tweets.

I try searching for Hobart users and a bunch of different words - fun, sexy, flirty, single, booty, dating, NSA – without much success. There are thousands of results from Melbourne and Sydney, but almost nothing in Hobart.

I get the same results when I make my searches a bit dirtier – horny, tits, pussy, cock. Nobody in Hobart is posting nude selfies or broadcasting their sex life, apparently.

I'm not surprised – Tasmanians are generally careful about keeping their private lives private - but when I search for 'fucking', there is one search result in particular that catches my eye.

Her name is SecretChloe.

Her profile pic is a cute pair of powder blue knickers, snug around her waist.

Her location is Hobart.

I read over her most recent public posts.

SecretChloe: Love laying back in bed on a rainy night getting my pussy eaten over and over

SecretChloe: The next 5 days off and I'm planning to not wear any panties the whole time!

SecretChloe: Such a nice day today, warm sunshine always makes me super horny!

It's probably a fake account, I tell myself… but I start following her anyway. If nothing else her pics, while anonymous, are damned sexy. And… I kind of like the idea of checking out the nude selfies of a girl that I could pass on the street.

I end up reading through her whole timeline.

SecretChloe: It's amazing how such little holes can take such big things!

I decide to reach out to her. It's almost 2am and

I'm alone, high, lonely, and using an anonymous X account.

What have I got to lose?

I agonise over what to write for nearly ten minutes.

She doesn't follow me, obviously, so it needs to be a public message. I definitely don't want to creep her out by being too aggressive, and I definitely don't want to come across as some desperate, simpering loser either.

I want to be friendly, approachable – and interested.

After a while, I type a reply to one of her posts. It takes a few attempts because my hands are shaking, but I finally get the words onto the screen. I stare at them for another minute, proofreading, debating whether or not to hit send.

Nobody else would have you.

I hit send.

TheUglyHusband: Ur pics are gorgeous. I love thinking that you could be the girl at my bus stop. You should post more x

My comment goes up, on my timeline and hers.

I immediately consider deleting it, but I don't. Instead, I take a deep breath and let the nervousness seep away.

It feels good. I'm safe, alone, and I just sent a message to an anonymous woman on the internet.

I'm definitely not the first person to do it… but it feels like a big deal.

Even if she doesn't respond, I've finally done something for myself – I've reached out, beyond my marriage, and touched the world.

Ironically, anonymously, I feel like a real person for the first time in years.

The horizon just reappeared, I can see it.

It's beautiful.

Chapter 15

I get out of bed early – early for a Sunday morning anyway – woken by my phone buzzing on the bedside table. There are two notifications on my *X* account.

SecretChloe has started following me.

And sent me a private message.

Half awake, I hold my breath until the message opens.

SecretChloe: Hey there, where in oz are you?

Holy shit.

I didn't think she would even follow me back, let alone initiate a conversation.

I let half an hour pass before I respond – I'm desperate not to look desperate.

TheUglyHusband: Hey girl I'm in Hobart. Where are you?

She doesn't reply straight away either.

But she does reply.

SecretChloe: Hobart too! On the eastern shore

TheUglyHusband: Hey cool. I'm city side. Guess ur not the girl at my bus stop tho lol. That's a shame x

SecretChloe: Would have been good hey. Is she a cutie?

TheUglyHusband: She sure is. Your pics are driving me insane… Would love to see more…

She doesn't reply for a couple of hours. By then I'm settling into the day, hanging with the girls, trying not to check my phone every ten seconds.

SecretChloe: Do they make your cock hard?

Well, they didn't… but it's getting hard now.

I've never sexted anybody, never talked about my dick with a stranger. It seems unreal.

TheUglyHusband: So fucking hard.

My head is light. My hands are shaking with excitement.

Claire and the girls natter away in the lounge-room.

Then…

SecretChloe: Are you married?

On the spot, I make the decision to be honest. Kind of. I don't have anything to lose.

There are so few people I can be honest with.

TheUglyHusband: More or less

SecretChloe: Lol

TheUglyHusband: Does that bother you?

SecretChloe: No. Is she good in bed?

TheUglyHusband: Yep. But…

SecretChloe: But what.

But what indeed.

I can't tell her my wife is cheating on me.

I want to be approachable, confident, interest-ing.

Not a desperate loser.

TheUglyHusband: But I need more lol.

No response.

Fuck. I've screwed it up already.

I *knew* I shouldn't have told her I was married, I knew I shouldn't have told…

My phone buzzes.

SecretChloe: How old are you?

Relieved, I respond without thinking

TheUglyHusband: 34. You?

As soon as I hit send, I wish I could take the question back. You just don't ask women how old they are, no matter what the situation is.

And I don't know if I'm too old, too young, too married, too creepy….

She doesn't respond.

Not after ten minutes, not after thirty minutes.

After a couple of hours I stop watching my phone. The elation I felt all morning is dissipating with every second that I don't hear from her.

The day winds out. I try to relax.

Chapter 16

M uch later, just after I've put the girls to bed and I'm waiting for them to fall asleep, my phone buzzes.

SecretChloe: Old enough lol

I grin like an idiot, sitting in the dark of my kid's bedroom.

I don't respond straight away - I don't want her to know how badly I want this conversation to continue.

I consider and discard a hundred different responses before I settle for a simple, single emoji - a smiley face.

I don't expect a response, and I don't get one.

But the butterflies dance in my stomach for the rest of the night.

Chapter 17

For the first time in a very long time, I wake up feeling great. The nervous fluttering in my belly starts even before I open my eyes.

The first thing I do is reach for my phone. I'm not even disappointed when there are no notifications.

My body is filled with a warm, glowing feeling, an excitement I barely recognise. It takes a little while to pinpoint it the feeling - I realise, while riding the bus to work, that it's the feeling of potential.

The feeling that something interesting could happen.

The feeling that life could take me anywhere, that the world could be my oyster.

Even the music on the bus's tinny radio sounds better.

I tell myself not to expect another message. Even though I badly want to talk to her again, I m happy to leave the ball in her court.

The fact that she spoke to me at all was a solid omen, one I'm taking a great deal of comfort from - it hinted that there might be, somewhere out there, a woman who could be interested in me.

Even if it was just an anonymous chat, I'm less alone in the world.

I'm not going to push it.

Chapter 18

B efore the bus even reaches the city, my phone
buzzes.

SecretChloe: Do you fuck other girls?

I want to cheer, I want to shout, I want to sing!
Excitement makes me bold.

TheUglyHusband: Sometimes. I wanna fuck
you

The response is almost immediate.

SecretChloe: What do you want to do to me?

I take some time on the next message, looking at
her pictures, reading her posts, catching her vibe.

TheUglyHusband: I wanna run my hands all
over your body while I slide my hard cock in and
out of your mouth.

Lol that should do it.

I've never sent anybody a message like that in
my life, not even Claire.

I don't think I've even *said* something like that
to anyone, ever.

It's exciting and feels almost dangerous.

I'm not even worried about whether she responds or not - I'm elated at my sudden boldness. Where the hell did *that* come from?

Before she can respond, I follow it up.

TheUglyHusband: Then I want to squeeze my cock into your little pussy and grind it.

I get off the bus, hoping nobody will notice the bulge in my pants.

As I'm walking through the Hobart bus mall, she comes back.

SecretChloe: Have you got a big cock? And lots of cum too?

TheUglyHusband: So I've been told. Your pictures are keeping me rock hard

SecretChloe: I love making guys hard. I love lots of cum too

I get to the office, nod hi to everyone and sit down at my desk as quickly as I can.

The room buzzes busily around me, but I barely notice as I compose my next message.

TheUglyHusband: Thinking about my cum on your lips. Pushing it into your mouth with my cock to make sure you get it all

She likes that, apparently.

SecretChloe: Smearing it all over my face! Then…

SecretChloe: Does your wife like her face

covered in your load?

TheUglyHusband: She likes it on her tits.

She had seemed to enjoy it, the one time it happened, many years ago.

TheUglyHusband: Where do you like it?

SecretChloe: I like it pumped inside me, shot over my face or filling up my mouth. I crave cock and cum

This conversation is fucking *unreal.*

My whole body is electrified.

My palms are sweating.

I'm rock hard and hoping my boss doesn't walk into the office to see me hunched over my phone.

TheUglyHusband: I wanna give them to you. i love cumming deep inside a tight pussy

SecretChloe: I love to feel a big fat cock push into my tiny pussy then fill it up with cum. How often do you fuck your wife? And how often do you fuck other girls?

TheUglyHusband: Not often enough.

SecretChloe: Could i see a pic of your cock and balls? I'm on my way to meet a guy right now!

Well then.

I've never taken a dick pic in my entire life.

I'm not about to take one while I'm sitting at my work desk. I'm not sure if I should take one at all… but I'm enjoying my boundaries being eroded, message by message.

TheUglyHusband: Lol later yeah. I'm at work. Send me a pic of your session, I wanna see you being fucked. Lucky bastard lol.

SecretChloe: We only have half an hour together so just a quickie today. Where do you work?

TheUglyHusband: In an open plan office, so I can't show you my cock… yet

SecretChloe: I just got in the guys car and on the way to the spot. Can't wait to see your dick.

TheUglyHusband: Can't wait to show you. Tell me what happens I'm so fucking turned on right now.

Chapter 19

I t's lunchtime, but there's no way I can eat. My stomach is flipping and flopping.

I go and sit in the park just outside my office. It's 30 degrees in the sun. I'm hot and bothered and I love it.

My phone buzzes.

SecretChloe: My pussy is full of cum!!!

And there's a pic.

My brain flips.

Her white undies are pulled to one side. Her smoothly shaven pussy, impossibly delicate, is spotted with thick pearls of semen. Her slit is tiny, her dark nail polish chipped away.

I stare at the photo for what seems like forever and another message comes in.

SecretChloe: Going home to mum like this! She has no idea what I get up to

TheUglyHusband: That's so hot I'm so fucking hard now. Your pussy is amazing, I want to kiss it then fuck it so hard

SecretChloe: Would you fuck me straight after another guy fucked me?

TheUglyHusband: I would take your mouth instead. Did he fuck you good?

SecretChloe: Yeah I bent over for him to pound me. Would you like to see your wife put on the spit?

TheUglyHusband: Sure. I'd rather watch her eat your pussy though.

SecretChloe: I know some older guys that would love to have her! Want to see her bent over with her ass up and her face buried in my pussy?

TheUglyHusband: Yeah just like that, putting her fingers in you, getting your pussy ready for my cock

SecretChloe: Has she had two cocks before?

TheUglyHusband: I don't think she has.

It's the truth. As far as I know.

Would my wife like being shared by two guys? Probably.

She probably does it all the time.

SecretChloe: is there anything you want to do to her that she won't let you?

TheUglyHusband: not much.

SecretChloe: do you pump her ass?

TheUglyHusband: once and it was great, but that's it. I wanted to fucking ram it.

SecretChloe: hold her hips and fuck her ass hardcore.

TheUglyHusband: you like your ass being fucked?

SecretChloe: yeah I love it

TheUglyHusband: would you like my tongue in your ass?

SecretChloe: fuck yes I would. That makes my pussy melt.

TheUglyHusband: I want to eat them both.

SecretChloe: do you eat your wife's ass?

TheUglyHusband: I would eat yours for hours. I would love to tongue fuck your ass while my cock is deep in your mouth

SecretChloe: I'd suck you dry as you ate my asshole. Cover your face in my juices

TheUglyHusband: I want to taste you. I'm so fucking hard right now. I would come so hard with your juices in my mouth

SecretChloe: My pussy gets so wet it drips

TheUglyHusband: Your pussy is gorgeous I want to see more

SecretChloe: It's getting more cock tonight now too!!!

TheUglyHusband: What are you gonna do with that cock?

SecretChloe: I'm going to suck it, lick it, guide it into my pussy and suck my juices off it

TheUglyHusband: Will you take his whole cock in your little mouth?

SecretChloe: I will try but I will gag!!! He has a big cock, it stretches me every time

TheUglyHusband: Would love to see your lips. Will you ride his cock or let him pound you?

SecretChloe: Probably both. I like to ride on top then suck his cock straight out of my pussy then ride it some more

TheUglyHusband: Oh fuck yeah. You like tasting yourself on his big cock?

SecretChloe: I love it!!! I always taste my juice

TheUglyHusband: Would you like your pussy being pounded from behind while you lick your juices off a fat cock?

SecretChloe: I would love that and I have done that too Have you ever tasted cum?

TheUglyHusband: lol have you had two guys coming in you at once?

SecretChloe: Yeah the most I've had is 4 guys at once and I have had that 3 times, same guys Wow.

TheUglyHusband: Wow

SecretChloe: They cum in me and cover my face. Make all holes full

TheUglyHusband: I wish I could see it. I need to cum so bad now. You're making my cock ache so much

SecretChloe: I want to see it. I have just had dinner and told the parents I'm going to a friends for a while!

TheUglyHusband: What are your panties like?

SecretChloe: I'm not wearing any!! I have some trousers and a t shirt on! But they won't be on for much longer

TheUglyHusband: Not just a quickie this time. Send me pics so i can cum

SecretChloe: I have got all night!!! Your turn to send me pics by the way

And then she's gone.

Can you die of horniness?

Chapter 20

I've never taken a dick pic before.

In fact I've never even *considered* doing it. If it's a rite of passage, then it's a passage I've never needed to go down.

The last time I was single, smart phones were still a year or two away from being invented. To send a dick pic you would need to get the photo printed at your local chemist then walk up to the girl you liked and hand it to them. Nobody did that. Did they?

Laying in bed, I read an article on *Reddit. Six Tips for Dick Pics,* written by a cam girl.

The tips are all straightforward – don't take a 'log' shot (a point of view photo looking straight down at your dick), don't forget to clean it up first (Jesus, really? You have to point that out? Some dudes must be gross) and don't use weird angles to try and make it look bigger because '*you'll actually make it look like a deformed pig leg'*.

The last point is discussed at length, with the writer at pains to point out that it's not the size that matters. She says that some guys put objects next to their cocks for a size comparison and it's the least sexy thing in the world – a hard cock with a can of deodorant pushed up against it

Instead, she advises, make it a *sexy* pic. Work with what you've got.

Take the photo from a low angle and make sure your balls are in the frame. Include a bit of thigh, or even a hand wrapped around the base. Make sure the light is complimentary.

I manage to wrangle the bathroom straight after work, thinking I could whip off a quick snapshot and keep the conversation with SecretChloe going.

Feeling pretty firmly at the edge of my comfort zone, I get my cock out and snap away. Using my phone camera means I can't see what I'm doing and the first couple turn out to be fleshy blurs.

There's a loud knocking on the bathroom door.

"Are you okay in there? What are you *doing?*"

Claire's voice makes me jump and I nearly drop my phone.

"Just having a quick shower, won't be a tick."

I lean over and turn the shower on.

"Okay. Dinner won't be far away."

She leaves me to it.

I get into the shower and edge. The shower head warms my balls, tickles along my shaft and I imagine SecretChloe running her lips along its length. By the time I turn the water off, I'm rock hard, almost ready to cum.

But when I pick the phone up, the rock starts to melt. Moving quickly, I put the phone into position – a low angle, looking up – and snap away.

A quick glance at the photos shows that the angle is bizarre – my knob is poking at the lens, sticking out like some kind of fleshy-coloured toadstool.

This is not sexy.

On the verge of giving up, I imagine my wife eating another woman's pussy, imagine slipping into her ass and then into her friend's mouth, imagine them kissing around my knob.

It works. A bead of cum blooms. I hold the phone up and take a photo.

Then I sit down on the edge of the bath and take a firm grip around the base of my cock, pushing my balls forward and lifting my thigh to fill the background.

I snap away.

By the time the family rumbles down the hallway, I'm dressed and ready for work. I sort them all out, kiss cheeks and walk down to the bus stop.

It's going to be a hot day.

Chapter 21

Once I'm nestled into the back seat of the bus, clear of any nosy over-the-shoulder readers, I open up my photos.

There are six in all – two of my knob balancing a white pearl of cum, four of the whole pillar and stones.

I pick the two best ones and do some editing – cropping some bath toys out of the background, correcting the colour, rotating to a better angle. I can't help but marvel about my phone for a moment; this amazing technology, capable of so much… and I'm using it to edit and transmit photos of my junk.

What a wonderful world we live in.

In the end, the photos are not too bad

I haven't heard from SecretChloe this morning. I wonder if she's pissed that I didn't send her a pic last night when she asked for one.

Now that I have photos ready, I get excited. As I

mentioned, I've never taken a dick pic before, let alone sent one to anybody, let alone sent one to an anonymous chick on the internet.

It gives me a buzz – she has no idea what I look like, but she'll see my cock. Even if she denigrates it, or laughs at it, or shows it to someone else, there's still an intimacy about it I wasn't expecting.

Still… I'm nervous about how she'll respond.

I want her to *want* it.

Without thinking, I write her a message.

TheUglyHusband: Woke up thinking about your pussy x

I attach the photo of my knob with the droplet of cum and hit send.

And there it is, in our conversation thread, a picture of my cock.

There's no going back now.

I'm elated. It feels great.

Even if she never speaks to me again, I've pushed through my comfort zone and done something daring, even dangerous.

I feel like dancing.

Then abruptly it dawns on me; it's not even 9am.

I've just sent her a dick pic uninvited, first thing in the morning.

My blood runs cold. While there are no rules about this sort of thing, I doubt that her insistence from yesterday afternoon has carried over through breakfast.

Shit.

I want to take the pic back, but I can't.

Now I just feel creepy.

I consider deleting the other photos, but the bus pulls up in the city and it's time to walk to work.

An hour later, I'm staring dejectedly out my office window.

She hasn't responded.

She didn't like it.

My timing was off.

My dick is too small.

She's probably off showing her friends the tiny…

My phone buzzes.

SecretChloe: Yum!!! I want to lick it up xxx

The relief is overwhelming. I sit back in my chair, my whole body relaxing.

I decide not to respond, even though it's tempting to send her the other photo straight away.

I'll keep it for when the time is right.

Chapter 22

Claire's Facebook account is still logged in on my laptop.

I've resisted checking her messages too often. I've already seen enough. It feels a bit like I'm prodding the wound.

And anyway, I've been distracted.

But I open it up tonight. Talking to SecretChloe has given me a bit more backbone to deal with whatever has been going on.

My wife is sleeping with somebody else. It isn't the end of the world.

Maybe she's been getting dick pics too and I can compare them with my own, sort of a dick-of-the-day club. Which one does my wife like today?

There are the usual conversations there; her mum, her besties, a couple of her colleagues and an old school friend or two.

And fourth or fifth in her list of conversations – that fucking grey shape again.

Ronnie.

She's been chatting to him.

I know I should just log out, I know I should just close the laptop and walk away. It's all over between us, I don't need to fucking know.

But curiosity gets the better of me.

Ronnie: you are soooo fukn hot xx so good to meet you on Saturday night

Claire: omg YOU are! xx sorry if I was a bit… drunk lol

Ronnie: no complaints here did you have fun?

Claire: It was amazing! I loved hanging with you x

Ronnie: SAME I could seriously watch you dance all night

Claire: lol you can watch me anytime

I hear a grinding sound. It's my teeth.

Ronnie: really lol don't you have a hubby

Claire: Lol maybe… yes…

Ronnie: Naughty girl. I hope you're okay? TBH I was so fucking turned on touching you.

Something flips in my stomach.

I should turn the laptop off, I should throw the fucking thing across the room.

But I don't.

Ronnie: sorry if that's too forward

Claire: no. I liked it a lot.

Ronnie: I'm glad.

Claire: i wanted more.

More? I lean in to the screen. She didn't fuck him after all?

Ronnie: Ngl I really wanted to take you home.

Clair: oh

Ronnie: oh?

Claire: I wish I could have come with you but…

Ronnie: But hubby. You live with him?

Claire: Yeah.

Ronnie: Cool. I wasn't sure if you were interested.

Claire: I was interested

Ronnie: Really. Was?

Claire: I'm still interested

She didn't fuck him *yet*.

I can't believe what I'm reading.

Ronnie: goooooood… me too

Claire: I loved having your hands on me. And you're such a good kisser.

My loving wife, making out with another man in some filthy fucking nightclub.

I'm not surprised, or relieved.

Just cold.

Who am I married to?

Who has my wife become?

Who have *I* become?

Claire: I really need somebody to make me cum

Ronnie: not hubby?

Claire: not hubby

No, not hubby.

Ronnie: Not gonna lie that's kinda fucking hot.

Claire: you're kinda fucking hot.

Ronnie: So can we hang out again sometime? Maybe after New Years?

Claire: I can't wait. I'm so fucking horny just thinking about it x

My mouth is hanging open.

I know it should hurt, that I should feel jealous, that I should try and bring a stop to all this, confront her, win her back... but I just feel tired.

There's a lump of stone in my heart where my wife used to be.

It's clear that I'm not enough for her. Maybe I never was.

It doesn't matter.

I don't care what she does.

She can't break me again.

I've got my own business to worry about.

Chapter 23

I wake up hard. Today is *the day*.

If I don't make a move with SecretChloe today, then it will probably never happen. It's my last day at work before the Christmas holidays. Christmas is the day after tomorrow, and I'll be in fucking Launceston with the family for at least a week.

And I don't want SecretChloe to lose interest. I don't want her to think I'm all talk.

I want to fuck her.

Today.

Right now.

I'm so goddamned randy that it's hard to think about anything else.

Claire wriggles in the bed but doesn't turn towards me.

I hate that my body still responds to her so easily. There is so much pressure in my groin.

We're not supposed to talk about what that

pressure can do to a man; it backs up into your brain, puts a filter over your vision and affects almost everything you do. It tips the balance of your humanity back towards the animal, the primal.

Any sensuality makes the brain bubble; any sexiness makes the balls ache. Sex changes from being a physical desire into a physical *need*. It's less about seeking pleasure and more about relieving pressure.

The effect is something akin to hunger in its urgency and aching - but it's a hunger to get something out. You might be able to go for days, weeks or even months without releasing that hunger – but in turn, it will consume you.

Still… I refuse to reach for my wife, despite her soft curves sighing on the mattress less than a foot away.

I'm not interested in being tolerated, in being pity fucked or placated.

I want somebody who wants *me*.

I get out of bed and head to the shower.

Chapter 24

I message SecretChloe as soon as I leave for work.

TheUglyHusband: Did you go to the beach this morning?

By the time I get off the bus, my whole body is thrumming with nervous energy. I think I'm getting hooked on this mixture of excitement and trepidation.

I feel so alive.

Today is the day.

SecretChloe: Yeah I sure did xox

I get off the bus and walk down to Salamanca. I'm early for work so I buy a coffee and sit down on one of the wooden seats near the Salamanca lawns.

It's time to push it.

TheUglyHusband: What are you up to tonight?

I'm waiting for a response, my hands trembling a little, when I hear my name being called.

Chapter 25

"Joey? Is that *you?*"

The words snap me back into this world. There is a smiling woman walking over to me.

I recognise her face. Her name is Lisa. And she looks wonderful.

I don't believe it's really her. It must have been ten years since I last saw Lisa, but here she is, smiling and kissing my cheek, sitting down for a chat.

I'm flabbergasted, delighted, in awe of the strange synchronicity of the universe.

Long ago, before I met my wife, Lisa and I had hooked up for one drunken night at the Uni Bar in Launceston. Her friend was seeing my friend, so we had been drinking together for most of the night when she had suddenly kissed me.

We had ended up back at her place in the early hours of the morning, naked under her bedroom window.

Her body had fascinated me; her breasts were small and delightfully firm, her shoulders muscled, her thighs strong. Her pussy was covered in fine, bushy red hair, remarkably untrimmed, delightfully damp.

It had been hot and heavy going... but we didn't actually have sex.

I remember her being naked, spread out beneath me, ready. I remember kneeling over her and rubbing my stiff cock against her slickness, ready to plunge in... when she told me to stop.

It doesn't matter how turned on you are, how badly your balls need to explode, how mindless your body has become in the moment... when a woman tells you to stop, you *stop*.

I'm randy, but I'm not a fucking animal.

I stopped. I didn't want to - and it wasn't easy - but I stopped.

And I was glad that I did.

She rolled me on to my back and kissed me deeply, her light pink nipples pressing against my shoulder. When the kiss broke off, she kissed me again, this time on the neck, then on the chest, then just above my navel.

When she took my cock into her mouth, my brain melted.

I was so fucking hard, her mouth so soft and warm. She licked and squeezed and tried to take it all in, moaning with desire, forcing my cock further and further into her throat.

I managed to gasp that I was about to cum, expecting her to finish me off with her hand, but instead she pushed her lips down to the very base of my cock and squeezed my shaft with her tongue.

I exploded, deep in her throat. Her soft mouth worked greedily, making sure it all came out.

It was the most intense orgasm I'd ever had.

She swallowed every drop, licked her lips and giggled at me shyly.

Fuck.

Afterwards, she told me that she had only been with one other guy and he had been younger than her. She wanted to sleep with me, but in the moment she had panicked. When I asked why, she told me I was too big - she was worried about it hurting.

In my euphoric, post-orgasmic state, it was pretty great news, even though it didn't make sense. I'm not small, but I'm definitely not huge. She would have been fine.

She must have come to the same conclusion - a few days later she sent me a message while I was driving to UTAS - *come over, I'm ready for you.*

I was so flustered I drove the wrong way down a three-lane city street and almost killed a bunch of drivers, including myself.

I didn't go over though. I can't remember why.

A few months later I heard that she had moved to India and I never saw nor heard from her again.

Until now.

We sit and chat and smile at each other and while she fills me in on the last few years of her life, my mind is racing.

We have unfinished business.

My phone buzzes a few times in my pocket.

Today is the day.

Lisa lives in the desert now, in the red centre. I can't help but notice the differences in her; the gentle, slightly awkward girl has become an impressive, strong woman.

She tells me about her time living with the mob up the top end, her trips to India, her published poetry.

I have a hard time sitting still; I want to grab her, kiss her, run my hands down her back.

It's the first time she's been back to Tassie in years, she tells me. She's flying out again on Boxing Day. Back to the distant desert.

She's writing a novel about dislocation, about a person's struggle to find a place where they really belong. I tell her about a local philosopher, Malpas, who I know has written books about the concepts of place and experience. She's never heard of him, so I offer to send her some links to his articles.

She asks for my number, so that she can text me her email address.

I give it to her, trying not to grin.

Then it's time to go. I'm already late for work.

I walk her back to the car she's borrowed from her parents. When we hug goodbye, she pulls me tight, like she doesn't want to let go.

I whisper to her.

"I still think about you sometimes, you know?"

And I kiss her on the cheek. We hold each other for a moment, then she is getting in the car and I'm walking to my office.

I wonder if she will text me.

Chapter 26

About 45 minutes later, she does.

Lisa: It was great to see you. My email is Lisa.acacia@gmail.com

Ok. I quickly google the professor l had mentioned, find a couple of articles and send the links to her email address.

Then I write a text.

Joe: Just sent you some articles. Was lovely to see you this morning x

I don't hit send just yet. Is this the right approach? I've never once in my life tried to seduce somebody who wasn't standing there in front of me.

The last time I was single - as a teenager - there were no mobile phones, no internet.

If you hooked up with somebody random, it was because you were drunk together at some party or club. If you were keen on somebody you didn't try to organise a hook up – you organised a date and hoped that it went well. You could spend days or even weeks letting somebody know you were interested and sussing out how they felt about you.

I've never even flirted with anyone online before SecretChloe.

But I'm determined to see this through.

Nobody would ever want to fuck you.

Well Lisa did, once.

Maybe she still does.

I don't want her to think I'm a sleaze, but I need to make a move.

Even if she dismisses me offhand, I need to start getting some confidence about this stuff.

I need to know that I can at least try and seduce a woman.

Being able to try this with somebody I actually know, somebody that I have been with before... this chance won't ever come up again.

The first step is to let her know that I'd like to see her again, so I add another line to the text message...

Joe: Just sent you some articles. Was lovely to see you this morning I wish we could have had longer to chat x

Her reply comes back immediately.

Lisa: Me too. I'm back in Kingston now. I just want to say thanks for saying what you did as you were leaving this morning. The last few days have been pretty rough and it was just what I needed to hear xx

Joe: I meant it. You made me feel incredible, I haven't forgotten xx

Lisa: Thanks. It's a pity you had to go to work, it would have been great to grab a coffee and catch up

Joe: For sure, I would really like that.

Lisa: I'm back in Kingston now, but I'll be in town tomorrow. Maybe we could have lunch or something?

I can't go anywhere tomorrow. School has finished for the year and I'll be at home with the girls while Claire is at work.

Today is the day.

Time to push it a little.

Joe: Sorry I'm heading to Launceston tomorrow for Christmas :(won't be back until the 29th. Do you come back to Tassie very often?

Lisa: Oh. That's a shame, it would have been nice to talk properly. No I only come back every couple of years for Xmas. Not sure about next year.

Talk properly. I'm not sure what to make of that.

While I'm considering my response, a X notification pops up - a direct message from SecretChloe.

SecretChloe: I have a threesome lined up for tonight!

Well then, that's settled. It's not going to happen with SecretChloe, not today.

Time to roll the dice.

Joe: Well... I was actually planning to go fishing tonight at the Woodbridge jetty. I think that's kind of close to you? You're more than welcome to come and chill. No pressure of course, I know you're busy catching up with family x

My hands are sweating.

I put my phone to the side and try to concentrate on work, to forget about it all.

She responds an hour or so later.

Lisa: Sounds nice. What time will you be there?

Joe: A bit after seven. I hope you can make it.

This time there's no reply.

The rest of the afternoon is an excruciating wait.

I don't know if she'll meet me there... and what will happen if she does.

I don't think about my wife at all.

Chapter 27

It's still early in the afternoon; I need to distract myself.

I open *X* and read through my conversations with SecretChloe. Before long, I'm turned on again, feeling trapped in my skin.

It's so damned hot in my office.

TheUglyHusband: Tell me what you're gonna do with those cocks

SecretChloe: I'm going to suck and lick them and take them in all of my holes

TheUglyHusband: Show me where you'll put the first cock

SecretChloe: Can't take pics at the moment cause I'm with my parents

TheUglyHusband: I'll be waiting x are your parents going out tonight?

SecretChloe: No but I told them I'm going out for a little bit. They guys will pick me up and we will go to one of their houses. What do you want them to do to me?

I'm rock hard, sitting at my desk, hoping like hell nobody comes in and spots me hunched over my phone. They'll think I'm looking at porn.

TheUglyHusband: I want you to strip for them and put your fingers in your pussy. Then one should eat your wet pussy while the other teases your lips with his cock. Take turns fucking your mouth for a while then put you on your back. One cock in your throat another pounding your pussy.

SecretChloe: You saying that has just made my pussy soaking wet

TheUglyHusband: Good. Then they should swap - one rubbing his shaft on your asshole while the other rubs his cock on your cheeks and lips

SecretChloe: My ass wants it

TheUglyHusband: He should slide his cock into ur ass while the other one makes you gag

SecretChloe: Oh fuck I want to finger myself right now. I'm in the car with mum and she has no idea what I'm up to lol. She has no idea her little angel craves big cocks

This seems like the kind of moment I've been waiting for.

TheUglyHusband: Lol should I send you a pic?
SecretChloe: Yes please

I'm so turned on.

I send her the second photo of my cock. I love

the idea of her being horny and seeing my hard dick, but there's still a touch of doubt about how she will react.

SecretChloe: I want your cock in my ass

Well, that's a pretty good reaction I reckon.

My junk is shifting, bulging against my pants. It's so fucking hot in here. My head is light and I can barely see straight.

TheUglyHusband: Anytime girl I wanna cum in your tight little asshole

SecretChloe: I need it now.

TheUglyHusband: I need to give it to you. Where are you?

Wherever she is, I'll go.

I'll walk out of my office, straight to the taxi rank on Collins Street and I'll go.

If she tells me any place in Hobart, I'll go there right now regardless of my plans with Lisa.

But she doesn't answer.

An hour later, I'm annoyed, deflated.

After idly toying with the idea of destroying my office, I try a couple of prompts.

TheUglyHusband: What would you do with my cock?

Nothing. It's almost the end of the workday anyway.

My balls are aching like hell, but that will be over soon.

One way or another.

Chapter 28

T he bus ride home is a blur.

I run inside, kiss the girls, wave to Claire and I'm gone again.

I chuck a bundle of fishing rods into the back of the car. For a few moments I consider taking Little K's car seat out of the back and stashing it in the shed, but I don't know how I would explain it to Claire if she happened to notice so I just get in and drive.

I pick up a six pack of Boag's Premium and a couple of condoms, feeling like a boss, then I drive south with the stereo blaring.

I don't know if Lisa will show up.

I don't know what I'll say to her if she does.

Will we spend a couple of hours sitting in awkward silence while I half-heartedly try to catch a few flathead?

What will she think if I try to sneak an arm around her waist?

If I try to kiss her?

Will she shame me for being a sleaze?

Would it matter if she did?

I get to the jetty just after seven, as promised, and my heart sinks.

The jetty is packed with people fishing in five or six small groups. There are even a few tourists wandering about. I should have guessed that it would be busy here, on a fine December evening just days before Christmas.

Even if Lisa does turn up, we'll have company the whole time. Awkward.

And... there she is.

She beat me here.

She's walking down the jetty between the fishermen, her expression disappointed. She's wearing all black and her red hair flips around in the breeze.

Feeling numb, I climb out of the car and wave hello.

She brightens and quickens her pace to meet me.

"Hey."

I smile as she stands in front of me. I have no idea what to say next... but it doesn't matter.

She steps into my arms as if she had never left them.

She turns her face up to mine and we kiss, softly

at first.

She is the first woman I've kissed, aside from my wife, in over fifteen years.

It feels *wonderful*.

My entire body thrums with electricity. Her lips are soft and inviting, unfamiliar, delicious.

When the kiss ends, she steps back, her cheeks flushed, and looks around at the jetty.

"There are lots of people here." She looks into my eyes. "Where else can we go?"

Chapter 29

Fifteen minutes later we pull into the carpark at Trial Harbour.

There's nobody else around, but the highway is only thirty metres away, just through the trees. The carpark follows the curve of the beach, around to where a floating dock bobs out into the bay. There's another car parked near the dock, so I pull up at the other end, near the BBQ area, and we climb out.

We can't keep our hands off each other.

I can tell that the stealth of our rendezvous is bemusing her, but she seems keen to go along with it.

She leads me to a smooth patch of grass near the beach and lays out the blanket I've hooked from the back of the car, sitting down and taking off her shoes.

"I've got some beer if you want one."

She laughs softly.

"You bought beer?"

'Well…" I shrug. "I usually bring a few down."

"You go fishing a lot?"

"Yeah. As much as I can."

"Do you ever actually fish?"

It's my turn to laugh.

"I'm a terrible fisherman."

"I'll have a beer. Thanks."

We sit down on the blanket next to each other. Cars whiz past on the highway just up the hill, but we ignore them.

Lisa has changed over the years of course - her body is slender and strong, her eyes are clear and far more direct. The shy, eager girl I knew is now a woman – a confident, well-travelled woman, tougher than I remember. The more we talk, the more she tells me about her life, the more impressed I am.

We kiss again and again, our hands exploring each other.

At one point a car pulls off the highway onto the road we had followed in, but it passes us without pause and continues along to the floating dock. She glances at it and bites her lip, smiling, then kisses me again.

Our bodies press hungrily together as the waves roll in nearby. It's cold, as any Tasmanian beach is when the breeze is up – but not cold enough to stop us slowly undressing each other, right there on the blanket.

"I want you naked." I tell her a few times. "I wanna make your whole body naked."

And soon she is. Most of my clothes have gone too.

She is beautifully feminine as she presses her warm skin against me. Her fine, red public hair is as bushy as I remember, and it feels delightful beneath my hand. I wonder at the unfamiliarity of her body, the hunger in her lips, the soft gasps she makes as I touch her wetness.

A light flashes along the beach at the other end of the carpark. I can make out two people getting out of it, walking along the jetty. It looks like two girls. They're far enough away to leave us alone.

Lisa lets out a little sigh as I stroke her clit with my fingertips. I can feel her warmth and I massage it, looking for more. When I find it, I slowly slip a finger inside.

Her body stiffens against me and her kiss becomes more urgent, more intense.

She lifts her hips to give my fingers more access and I slide another one in beside the first. Her pussy is deliciously warm and my palm is already wet as she pushes against it.

Her hand reaches for me, pushing my boxers down, wrapping around my hard cock.

She kisses her way down my chest, not wasting any time.

Her lips are soft and her tongue is firm as they work their way up my shaft. She takes it into her mouth, drawing me in, looking up to smile with her eyes.

My mind is blank. It's the first time anyone other than Claire has touched me in a very long time and it feels *fucking incredible*.

I brush her hair out of her eyes and wrap it up in my hand, gently thrusting into her mouth. She wriggles her head, pushing it in further. I'm groaning so loudly, but the sound is lost in the thump of the waves.

She wriggles off me and sits up, face flushed, her pretty nipples stiff.

"Do you have a condom?"

I freeze. Shit.

I do have a condom – in the car. I tell her so. Her laugh has more than a hint of frustration.

"Well go and *get* it!"

I sit up. Cars are still whizzing past on the highway behind us, but they can't see down here. Around at the jetty, the girls are dancing about. At least, one of them is.

"Go on!"

She laughs again as I stand up, naked, my cock swinging through the evening air.

To hell with it.

I clamber across the grass, up the little slope and across to the parking bay. The car is unlocked, thank Christ, and the condoms are in the side pocket where I had stashed them earlier.

I scruff them and scurry back down to her.

She claps as I come back and I can't help but grin. I don't think I've ever been naked in public before, but the evening air feels great on my skin.

It's only when Lisa pulls me back against her warm body that I notice; I'm not hard anymore. I'm so amazingly turned on that I didn't even notice.

She notices it too, of course. She smiles.

We kiss, long and deep, and I tickle her pussy again.

"Let me kiss you here," I whisper into her here.

She bites her lip, her eyes shining, and I start to push her down… but she pushes me back, and kisses me again.

"Let me get above you," she whispers.

My naked body feels exposed as I lay back, half off the blanket and half on the scrubby grass, but I forget all that as she kneels above me, placing a smooth thigh either side of my head.

Her fine, red hair tickles my nose as she lowers her pussy onto my tongue.

She moans, loudly, and I run my hand over her

breasts. My tongue explores her as she grinds at my chin. Her hand is firm on the back of my head and she looks down at me with her lips curling as she bucks her hips against my lips, faster and faster.

I spread her open, push my tongue in and around and her eyes roll back in her head as she thrusts against my face.

Suddenly she spasms, once, twice, twice again.

My face is soaked in her sweet liquid. I bury myself in her and slowly lick, pushing my tongue out to make it as fat as I can. She gasps again, then draws away.

"Fuck me," She pants, laying down on her back. "Fuck me now."

I kneel above her, ready to go… well, almost ready.

I'm still only at half-bar, despite how sexy it was to have her ride my face. I try to cover it by fumbling around with the condom, but it droops even more.

She sees what's happening and leans up, taking me into her mouth again.

This time it's me that gasps; she works it hard and within seconds I'm stiff again.

She takes her mouth away and smiles at me, stroking my revived hard on with her hand, leaning back and opening her…

Suddenly I'm coming, without warning, without reason.

My heart sinks. My stomach shrivels.

I cum on Lisa's arm.

"Oh!"

She takes a firmer grip, squeezing out a bit more, but there's no pleasure in it for me.

I'm mortified.

What. The. Actual. *Fuck.*

"Oh shit!" The words feel so weak in my mouth. "What the hell?"

She looks up at me, confused, clearly trying to hide her disappointment.

Suddenly the night feels colder.

I'm still kneeling upright. Stupid. I lower myself onto the blanket, feeling very naked.

"Are you okay?" She asks, uncertain.

"Yeah. A bit embarrassed. I'm sorry."

"Don't be." She pulls me close again, wraps her arms around me. "I had a very good orgasm. A strong one."

It was a kind thing to say. I don't know how to respond.

We sit there in silence for a while.

"You're married now, aren't you?" She asks eventually. There is no judgement in her voice.

"Yeah."

"Is this the first time you've…"

"Yeah. We've been together a long time."

"But it's not going well."

"Things haven't been great. When I saw you this morning…"

She smiles again. "I always regretted not sleeping with you."

I kiss her. "And I always wanted to get you naked again."

"Are you going to leave her?"

"I think so. I don't know."

She nods. "It's complicated."

"Yeah."

"You don't love her anymore?"

I try not to sigh. My hard on is long gone. At least the wind has dropped off.

"It's hard. She… she can be intense. She gets angry."

"And she takes it out on you?"

"A few weeks ago she was pissed off at her friend's husband and she said to me *'I know you're not cheating on me because nobody else would have you. Nobody would ever want to be with you.'*"

"Oh my *god!*"

"I took it pretty badly."

"Joe, that's so wrong. She's so wrong." Lisa squeezes my arm, shaking her head. She seems genuinely angry. "Nobody has the right to say that to you."

"Thanks Lisa. " I go to kiss her on the cheek, but she leans away.

"I'm serious. I remember what you were like at uni. You were cocky and loud and you didn't care what anyone thought. And you were so fucking *sexy*."

"A long time ago."

"So who are you now?"

I can't speak. I don't have an answer.

The way she has just cut straight to the heart of it has thrown me off tilt.

Her voice is gentle.

"Joey. You're a six-foot tall, good-looking, decent guy. Nobody should treat you like that. There's nobody in the world you need to answer to. Except yourself."

I nod, not trusting myself to speak.

It's the kindest thing anybody has said to me in a long time.

"It's true."

I run my fingernails down her cheek, along her neck, over her chest and to her pink nipple.

"I want to thank you." I whisper to her, holding her eyes as I bend my lips down to her nipple. "I want to thank you so hard…"

"Also," she giggles. "You talk like you're in a porno."

I push her on to her back, stretch her body out

111

beneath my hands.

"My favourite pornos," I tell her as I spread her knees apart again, "...are the ones where they're next to the beach."

"Let's make one of those."

She wriggles beneath me. My stiffness knocks against her and she gasps.

"Let's make it *slowly*."

And we do go slow. For a while at least.

We lose ourselves in the rhythm of the waves and make our own warmth on that cold, dark beach.

Chapter 30

Later, much later, I'm sitting at home on the balcony, freshly showered, smoking a joint under the stars.

I feel great.

I feel *new*.

It's amazing, the difference a few days can make.

My phone buzzes. *X*.

SecretChloe: I'm so sore!!!

I smile into the darkness.

Chapter 31

And then it was Christmas.
I don't want to talk about Christmas.

Chapter 32

The Boxing Day boredom is killing me.

After our massive fight yesterday, Claire stays at her parent's house with the girls while I go and visit my dad. I like visiting Dad; he'll chat for ten minutes and then get back on with whatever it was he was doing, leaving me to my own devices.

And my device is getting a fair workout - I'm checking *X* every ten minutes in case SecretChloe shows up.

She doesn't. I haven't heard from her since the other night, but I'm not surprised. It's the holidays after all.

Lisa has disappeared back into the desert, taking my renewal with her. I don't want to lose the feeling, *can't* lose the feeling of being desired, of being free, of being in control.

And after yesterday's drama, I'm ready to be shoved out of my comfort zone again.

I check out some of the hook-up websites that

I've heard of, but all of them want money first, thanks, with no real evidence that they have any local members.

I run a *Google* search - casual sex in Launceston.

More ads for 'premium' dating sites, more links to paywalls… and a couple of results from a site called *Locanto*.

I click on the top one and hold on to my hat.

There are dozens of ads in the 'casual encounters' section, all located in Launceston. Most of them are from men looking women, men for men, men looking for groups of men… but there are a few ads from women as well.

With little else to do, I go through all the ads posted by women. Half an hour later, I've responded to six of them.

I get six replies. All of them contain links to an *'age verification site'* – which to me roughly translates as *'potential identification fraud'*.

My initial excitement quickly dies away. None of the responses are real. Does that mean none of the ads are real?

I read through them all again, more thoroughly this time, looking at the men's ads for comparison. A few include an obviously fake email address, like the women's ads… but a couple simply say *'meet me at x at x o'clock'*.

One of them reads:

25M looking for random NSA fun with F,M, MM or FF. City Park, near the train, anytime after 10pm.

City Park. Oh the songs they've sung.

When I was a teenager in Launceston, the City Park was known as a place for cruisers - gay men - to hook up. Since it was resting on the edge of the CBD, five minutes' walk from a couple of Launceston's larger nightclubs, it was also the go-to place for clubbers to consummate their own drunken romances.

On any Friday night in summer you could find half a dozen disparate groups scattered through the park, all exploring their own particular penchant - groups of underage drinkers, groups of pot-smoking vagabonds, groups of uni students transferring from the party to the club (or vice-versa), groups of burly men putting their fists inside other men's assholes.

It was seedy, but nowhere near as dangerous as the grownups made it out to be.

As a teenager I'd had my own experiences of City Park – drinking cheap wine, or taking acid for the first time and wandering through the trees, or hanging out and playing stoned hacky-sack on Spring afternoons.

I also took a girl from a nightclub there once.

It was after midnight. A bunch of us had been at the Pavilion, a meat-market nightclub on the edge of the city. I was fall-down drunk; Ruth Bird was a horny, lovely looking girl with wide vacant eyes who was happy to follow my lead.

I lead her to the park and some of our friends tagged along.

No shelter, no shadows, no attempt at all to be private - we simply lay down on the soft grass and went for it while our friends laughed, shrieked and threw pebbles at my butt.

We had been at it for a while when Smithy tapped me on the shoulder.

"Joe…"

"Fuck off!" I shouted politely.

"Erm… dude. We need to go."

"Seriously man, what the…"

I turned around to rip him a new one… and the words died in my throat.

There were men everywhere.

They were standing in a loose circle around us, watching us, a pack of hyenas.

A couple of them had their cocks out.

Smithy was wide-eyed.

"We gotta get the fuck out of here now, Joe."

He was freaking out, and rightly so.

"Piss off, Matthew!" Ruth Bird giggled from beneath me.

She clearly hadn't noticed our audience.

I clambered off, reefed my pants up, then quickly

covered Ruth as well. She sat up, annoyed and confused, grass stuck to her hair.

"What the hell do you…" her words trailed off as she saw the silhouettes of anonymous men. She gasped and clutched at my arm, panicky.

"Joe?"

I heard a deep, anonymous voice rumble.

"Fuck. She's gorgeous. So *young*."

Smithy kicked my leg.

"Let's get the fuck out of here!"

To his credit, he waited until both Ruth and I were standing before he bolted.

I put my arm around Ruth and marched her across the grass.

For one awful, terrifying moment I thought the circle of men was going to close on us… but we walked without pause and two dark shapes moved aside to let us through. I was considerably taller and wider than either of them and I think that was our saving grace.

If the men had realised that I was just a kid too… I doubt they would have let us go quite so easily.

The hyenas would have fed.

While it was frightening at the time, the experience left little lasting impression - I was a drunk teenager after all.

And now, if anything, remembering Ruth Bird's naked hips on the lawn only increases my curiosity about what goes on at the park after dark.

Nobody would ever want to fuck you.

Really? Fucking *really*?

Let's find out.

Chapter 33

I wave Dad goodbye and drive down to the City Park just before 10pm.

The city is quiet. I leave my car in a nearby street and skip the obvious entrances by jumping the fence near the old train park.

The park seems deserted, but it's so big that at this time of night that I can only see about a quarter of it. The entire boundary is lined with bushy gardens, and tall trees make huge shadows over the sweeping lawns.

I fade into the shadow of the nearest tree, sit down, wait.

Nothing happens.

I roll and smoke a cigarette. Then another. And another.

A couple of tourists walk quickly through the park, but that's it.

Then I spot the guy.

He's sitting on the base of an ornamental cannon,

just a bit up the hill from where I'm reclining on the grass.

If he's spotted me, he's not showing any sign of it. I can see the orange glow of a cigarette in his hands. Surely he can see mine too.

I wait.

After a while, the guy gets up and stretches.

There's no way of knowing if he is the one who posted the ad on *Locanto*… but it's safe to assume that he is. Apparently, there are no takers.

Hitching his pants up, he walks down the hill, following the path, and disappears deeper into the park.

I wait.

After about ten minutes, he finishes his loop and sits back down underneath the cannon.

Still no takers.

I don't light another cigarette.

I wonder if the guy has somebody at home, waiting for him, wondering where the hell he is.

He stands and sets off on another circuit.

I wait until he's out of sight, then beat a quick retreat back over the fence.

I get in my car and drive to Claire's parents' house.

We acknowledge each other awkwardly. Her parents chat away, trying to brush over the obvious tension.

She gets me a beer.

We watch TV in silence until it's time to go to bed.

Chapter 34

I'm heading back to Hobart by myself.

I've had enough of the tension, the tears, the stiff conversations. I've had enough of checking my phone every ten bloody seconds.

The need to touch and be touched is overwhelming.

I can't stop looking at *X*, can't stop thinking about SecretChloe. If she suddenly invites me over, I don't want to be 200 fucking kilometres away.

So I'm driving back. I don't care how it looks, or what anybody thinks.

I drop in to say bye to Dad. He slips me $200.

"Go and get drunk. See your friends. Get out and have some fun, for fuck's sake."

I promise him that I will.

The day is sweltering, so I drive shirtless, another thing I've never done before. It feels great. I feel so free. It's funny how much difference a few small changes can make.

I pull in at Campbell Town for an iced coffee and a joint, laying down in the shade of a huge gum tree in the park with my phone.

SecretChloe: Got a ticket for Falls Festival! Only my second time going

The post, from an hour ago, is accompanied by a porn .gif of a young woman in the doggie position pushing herself back onto a seated man's cock. The caption;

SecretChloe: How I got the ticket lo_.

Damn.

I'll be home alone for the next three nights, but she's going to the festival for two of them.

I send her a message.

TheUglyHusband: Falls eh?

SecretChloe: I went last year and I loved it! Are you coming?

Of course not. I've never been to the big music festival that happens every year an hour out of Hobart. It's a depressing thought.

But it has been sold out for months. There's no way I could get a ticket now.

I kick an empty coke can as I walk back to the car.

TheUglyHusband: Maybe next year.

SecretChloe: Cool. It's so much fuuuuuun!

TheUglyHusband: Lol I bet. Did you fuck

anyone last year?

SecretChloe: Just one guy. This year I'm going to fuck them all!

The car's too hot.

I should just turn around and drive back to Launceston.

I should try and patch things up with Claire and hope for a better New Year.

But I keep driving.

Chapter 35

I'm home alone, sitting in the sun, smoking weed even though it's barely 10am.

I fire up my laptop – Claire's account is still logged in to *Facebook*. I see the monosyllabic messages we've traded, and some extraordinarily long conversations with her girlfriends that I decide not to read... and a recent message from Ronnie.

Ronnie: Merry Xmas sweetie xxx

Claire: and to you, sexy xxx having fun out there?

Ronnie: NO! Nothing but family stuff the last week or two. I love them but GOD I could use a night out... and some cuddles.

Claire: Oh god, me too.

Ronnie: Hubby not performing :P

Whoever this fucking guy is, I want to kick his ass.

Claire: We've been fighting. He's home alone,

I'm at my parent's house.

Ronnie: Oh that's no good. Not.. not because of me?

No, you goddamned jerkoff. She hasn't mentioned you.

And neither have I.

Claire: Lol no he he's just… god I don't know. He drives me up the fkn wall.

Ronnie: He's not meeting your needs?

Claire: Not even close

Ronnie: Is he small? Down there?

Claire: No, but he's just so… boring! So… so…

Ronnie: Vanilla?

Claire: YES! Exactly!

Ronnie: That's a shame.

Claire: And he's let himself go the last few years and I just want some fucking excitement in my life and… god, it sounds terrible. I'm terrible.

Ronnie: It's okay to have needs, we all do.

Claire: You don't seem very vanilla

Ronnie: I'm definitely not vanilla lol

Claire: Do you think you could make me cum? Like really hard?

Ronnie: you're so fukn naughty!!!! I love it!! And yes I would. Many times

Claire: not that naughty lol

Ronnie: o rly? What would Mr Vanilla think about you talking to me?

Claire: Who gives a shit. Do you mind that I'm married?

Ronnie: Ngl it's pretty hot. Naughty girl

Claire: lol is it? I guess so

Ronnie: He's an idiot if he doesn't appreciate his hot sexy wife.

Claire: He used to be so much fun. Now he's just… meh

Ronnie: So where was he while we were dancing?

Claire: omg lol he was stoned at home, stuffing his face with doritos

Ronnie: hmm I thought you'd be married to a total bull

Claire: maybe once upon a time. Not anymore.

Ronnie: he doesn't fuck you anymore?

Claire: no he does. Sometimes. And it's good… sometimes…

Ronnie: but?

Claire: but… it's always the same. And… he doesn't look after himself. sometimes im kind of grossed out. God that sounds terrible dcesn't it

Ronnie: no babe, if he's not making you happy then… that's what I'm here for xx

Claire: He's so fucking oblivious ☹

Ronnie: I don't think so bb you just have needs. We all have needs. If hubby can't meet them then you gotta let somebody else. You wouldn't be the first. And your secret's safe with me xx

Claire: You must think I'm awful

Ronnie: No way babe, ur a fucking goddess

Claire: xxx

Ronnie: lol poor hubby.

Claire: Poor me

Ronnie: Poor you. I'm here to help, whenever you want x

I'm laughing so much that I could cry.

Chapter 36

SecretChloe: Had 3 different fucks yesterday, I've had a cold shower now I'm ready to go again. I love this festival!! xx

TheUglyHusband: I wish I was there. What are you wearing?

SecretChloe: Just a little dress thing and a bra...
... That's all

I leave her to it.

I'm home alone with time to kill, which is extraordinarily rare.

Funnily enough, I don't feel alone with my phone in my pocket. It's never out of reach. I'm finding more people to follow on X; mostly escorts, strippers and cam girls, but also a few anonymous women who post naked selfies or talk smut with whoever piques their interest.

All in Australia; none in Tasmania. I keep looking.

After a while I come across a woman in Melbourne. Miss_Innocent_Au.

Her account is only a week or two old, with less than 100 followers. She's posted three selfies so far - two of her bikini body sunbathing next to an expensive looking pool and one duck face.

The bikini body is impressive, so I click *Follow*.

I'm not used to having so much free time. I put it to use by exercising as much as I can. I push up, sit up, chin up, stand up and run. The first time I jog up and down Risdon Road it feels as though I'm going to pass out. But I don't. I rest for a while, then launch into squats.

My limbs burn, I'm out of breath and sweating like nobody's business, but it feels great. It feels like I'm actively changing my life with each rep. By the early evening my body feels broken, which is fine by me.

I wish I could go out, but in the nethertime between Christman and New Year's Eve, I would be out alone. Roger messages and invites to me a party at his house the following week, and I honestly can't fucking wait.

I keep tabs on Miss_Innocent_Au. Her posts are increasingly revealing photos as the day goes on. Her pics get more explicit, she gets more and more followers.

Anonymous men egg her on to post more, their comments dripping with the slimy stench of loneliness. Some of them toady up to her with comments about how gorgeous she is. Other's talk about what they would do with her body. Others try and engage her in dirty talk, which seems to be the only thing she actually responds to.

We learn that her husband is away.

We learn that she likes to show off for the boys.

We learn that she has three men coming over once the sun goes down.

The hyenas drool.

I don't message her but I'm rapt, along with everyone else.

By 9.30 that night, she has close to five hundred followers, all of them men, all of them whining for more.

After teasing us for a couple of hours, she posts another two photos - the first one is of the black panties she's been showing off all afternoon, only this time there is a man's hand down the front of them.

The second is photo of Miss_Innocent_Au with a condom-covered cock in her mouth.

The crowd goes wild.

Soon after, she posts another photo. She's wearing a new outfit - a sheer summer dress that barely covers her. She thanks her husband's friend for taking the photo once he was finished with her.

Then she tells us that the other two men have

arrived and that she'll be offline for the rest of the night.

The hyenas keep circling for a couple of hours, but she's gone.

Chapter 37

The idea of spending New Year's Eve alone is more depressing than I'm willing to contemplate.

For most of my adult life, NYE has been a marker, an event, something to look forward to for weeks beforehand and to talk about for weeks afterwards. The highlight of every summer. A spiritual celebration of life and the relentless passage of time. It's more special than a birthday; it's everybody's birthday.

It is also, of course, a prime opportunity to get wasted and lose it for a while.

Claire and I have always been together on NYE. We've always kissed on the stroke of midnight.

But this year I'm at home, alone. Claire and I haven't made any plans, for the first time in our relationship, because we've barely been speaking for weeks.

She's in Launceston with the girls. I'm in Hobart

with the car.

And even though I can't stand her right now, even though I don't want to be anywhere near her, the fact that we're even considering spending New Year's Eve apart is a startling indicator of how bad things have become between us.

If we don't start the New Year together, it seems pretty unlikely that we'll finish the year together.

The symbolism whacks me relentlessly.

Am I still a part of the family?

What sort of juju will I take into the New Year?

Where can I get wasted?

I know one thing – I'm not staying at home alone. If there was ever a night made for hooking up, it was New Ye…

My phone rings. It's Claire.

"Hey." Even from a single word, I can hear the trepidation in her voice.

"Hey."

"So… it's New Year's Eve."

"Yeah."

"What time will you get back up here?"

"Oh."

Oh. I wasn't expecting that.

"You want me to come back?"

There is a pause.

"Of course." There is a slight tremble in her voice that only I could ever notice. "I assumed you would. We have to spend New Year's Eve together. As a family"

"Yeah."

"You'll come?"

"Yeah.

"Good." The relief in her voice is obvious. "What should we do?"

"No idea. Anybody having a party up there?"

"Nobody that I know. But… my cousins do this thing every year, they go camping with a few other couples… I'm sure they wouldn't mind if we tagged along. We could go with them?"

"Sure, I guess." It's better than nothing. Her cousins are solid drinkers, country folk. I wonder who the other couples are.

"Okay. Good. I… we'll see you soon."

"Okay."

Chapter 38

I load the car up again and drive back to her parent's place in Launceston.

With unusual efficiency, we bundle the girls into the car and drive further north, just beyond Lilydale. I set up our tent amongst the caravans and swags. I tread carefully.

Surprisingly enough, it's not a terrible night. Claire and I don't talk much to start off with, but her cousins and their friends are relaxed and easy going. As the wine flows and the fire crackles, we settle into an amiable rapport.

We all get stuck into the booze. We drink and talk shit. There are lots of laughs.

Every now and then I catch Claire watching me with an unreadable expression.

Little K falls asleep on my lap until it's time for the countdown. We shout the numbers and Little K sits up, blinking, while Big M and the other kids jump around wildly and the adults swing their drinks from side to side.

As a cheer goes up around our campsite, Claire leans over and kisses me, first on the cheek, then on the lips.

We look into each other's eyes for a moment.

"Happy New Year," she whispers. "I love you."

Nobody else would be with you.

I nod and mumble something back. I feel sick.

Was I really considering spending New Year's Eve away from my wife? Away from my daughters?

Just to fuck some stranger?

What's happening to me?

Happy New Year.

Chapter 39

SecretChloe: Back home now all cleaned up lol How was your New Year's x

TheUglyHusband: Mmm dirty girl lol. Was ok, camping up North - driving back to Hobart now x

SecretChloe: Got absolutely pounded yesterday

TheUglyHusband: Did you end up on the spit? Poor little pussy i hope its ok lol Wanna tell me about your favourite fuck down there?

She doesn't reply, so I pull back out onto the highway.

Claire and I are on better speaking terms now, but we both thought it was a good idea for me to come home for a week while she stays at her parents with the girls.

Everybody needs a break. And space. This will be our summer holiday.

When SecretChloe finally replies, I park in a rest

stop on the side of the Midlands Highway. I'm not in any rush to get back home. It feels like I've got all the time in the world to spend as I please, and it seems pretty luxurious.

SecretChloe: Yeah on the spit a couple of times. I met a guy so him and his mates fucked me for like two hours

TheUglyHusband: Mmm sounds nice. Lucky dudes lol. Best bit? I love thinking about your body being used

SecretChloe: The best bit of it was thinking that they was all finished and another guy would come into the tent!!

TheUglyHusband: And you would start sucking the next cock?

SecretChloe: Yeah or he would just start fucking me straight away!

I drive again. The day is hot, the music loud.

I think about SecretChloe, tents, cocks.

Chapter 40

There's something I love about waking up in an empty bed.

The day seems to have so much more potential, like I could go anywhere, do anything, be anyone.

Of course there's a brief melancholic sting when I remember that I'm not seventeen anymore… but that passes quickly.

As soon as my eyes adjust to the new day, I'm reaching for my phone.

Even though she hasn't messaged, the idea of SecretChloe being out there – the idea that there might be other SecretChloes out there - is enough to make me leap out of bed.

While I probably have at least a few days to myself, I'm acutely aware that this languorous solitude won't last forever and I'm determined to make the most of it.

I crank up the stereo, drink a waterfall of coffee and roll a fat joint.

Tasmania is apparently having its hottest summer in a billion years and the timing couldn't be better. I spend the morning outside, cleaning and doing long-overdue chores and working out.

Nothing unusual... mostly.

I decided not to wear any clothes today.

I'm letting it all hang out in the backyard, which *isn't* completely private. The sunshine feels amazing on my skin, as though it's touching it for the first time ever. On some parts, it probably is.

I can't remember ever feeling so liberated, so free to do whatever I choose.

There is very little in this world as satisfying as spending a hot afternoon smoking joints naked in a paddle pool under the shade of your own tree. I keep a keen eye on the gaps in the front fence to see if any of the lovely ladies that live on my street walk past.

None do. Probably a good thing.

I do more chores and work out. My stereo makes the windows rattle from morning till well after dark. I take two baths and stream porn directly to our big TV in the loungeroom. I smoke weed all day and eat dinner at midnight.

But despite spending all day alone, I'm more social than I have been in a long time. My phone is my lifeline to the universe. I strike up conversations with strangers online, talk filth with anonymous women, argue with eggs about *Interstellar*. I barely eat.

I almost don't recognise myself.

I'm so goddamned, painfully, mind-numbingly horny.

Roger's party is only a couple of days away and I can't wait. I'll take a house party over a nightclub every time, thanks.

It'll be my first night out since all this started.

And there will be a woman there, Ellie, who has tried to flirt with me more than once despite my wedding ring.

Ellie is a traveller, friendly and open, a performance artist on the festival circuit, here for January then away again, chasing summer around the globe.

I first met her at Roger's party last year. We had talked about MONA for a bit, then taken turns sniffing on a bottle of Amyl Nitrate when it was passed to us. She had an uncomplicated face and a dancer's legs and we had hit it off. I'm looking forward to seeing her again.

I wonder if she would take me home, given the chance. A one-night stand.

The idea makes my entire body flush with excitement.

It's unlikely to happen.

And besides, most of the people at the party are

friends with Claire, or at least know that I'm a long-termer.

But do I care about that? I don't even know anymore.

Chapter 41

SecretChloe: What are you up to today?

TheUglyHusband: Heading to a bash in Sandy Bay this arvo. Until then, sitting around thinking about your ass

SecretChloe: Fucked your wife lately?

TheUglyHusband: I haven't seen her in a while

SecretChloe: Where has she been?

TheUglyHusband: Up north for xmas. I bailed and came back to Hobart

SecretChloe: Haha you must be a bit horny then

TheUglyHusband: Hah a bit. A lot.
Honestly it feels like I'm dying. Can blue balls be fatal? Let's find out.

SecretChloe: Any girls at sandy bay later on?

TheUglyHusband: There's one girl I definitely want to fuck at the party.

SecretChloe: Who is she

TheUglyHusband: Some random friend of

my mate. We've been flirty before, but i wasn't hooking up with people at that stage. I reckon I can get her to go for a walk

SecretChloe: How old is she

TheUglyHusband: I'm not sure. Younger than me

SecretChloe: I'm guessing she is hot, do you have a pic of her

TheUglyHusband: Nah. Maybe later lol

SecretChloe: Sneak a pic with her lol What's her name

TheUglyHusband: Everyone calls her Ellie. Probably short for something

SecretChloe: Cute name. You want to see my ass?

TheUglyHusband: You know I do. I wanna see all of you

SecretChloe: I might take some later. And I think my pussy has recovered after falls now too

Is that an invitation? It kind of feels like one. I get the feeling that if I were to push it now, if I were to ask her to meet me later, then she would.

But, for once, I've got places to be.

Of course... if she invites me over then I'll ditch my plans and go to her.

But she doesn't.

Chapter 42

I strut my way down to Roger's party, wearing only a singlet and shorts, collecting a bottle of gin and a six pack of beer on the way.

The evening is warm and Hobart is lively. Sandy Bay's huddle of restaurants and cafes are overflowing, students walk this way and that carrying groceries or alcohol, taxis zoom past on their way to somewhere else.

Roger's front door is wide open so I march on in and follow the music through to the backyard.

"Joey!" Roger calls from the barbeque he's managing. "You're allowed out for the night! Hoo-fucking-ray!"

"Mate, I'm off the leash. So fucking far off the leash."

"Looking for a new owner?" Marco pipes up from his picnic chair. He's using scissors to chop a big marijuana bud into the small bowl balanced on his knees.

"Nup. I've gone feral."

"Five minutes off the leash and you'd catch rabies from some scabby bitch." Marco shakes his head.

"She'll fuckin' put you down, Joey!" Roger warns me mockingly. "Hey where's Joe? *Oh* he's gone to live on the farm."

"He's floating down the river in a hessian sack." Marco adds.

"Joe? You've not gonna get neutered are ya?" It's Phil, emerging from the kitchen door with a tray of cheap sausages. "Cause I've already cooked the other boys up."

He waves the sausages at me. Roger and Marco laugh.

It's just the four of us for the first hour or so, but as the sky gets darker more and more people show up. By nine o'clock there are about two dozen of us sitting around in the small back yard.

Roger's stereo is blasting *Everything Everything* into the evening air. There are six or seven conversations happening at once. Everyone has a drink in their hand and every second person is rolling a cigarette.

I love nights like this. I used to live for nights like this.

Roger knows a lot of interesting people. About half of the party is made up of guys and girls I've

149

known for many years, but the rest are new faces.

While at least one of the girls I've known for many years would be up for a sneaky affair – I think anyway, Rachel has always been very touchy-feely with me and is quite open in her dislike of Claire – it's not worth the risk. There are few secrets in a small group of friends like this.

I wonder how many of them know about Claire and Ronnie.

Ellie arrives just before ten with another girl. The other girl – Maddie - looks a lot younger than her, but they're clearly good friends. Maddie is tall and thin with rich black hair and a sharp, reserved face. She's very attractive, but gives off an unmistakable aura of unapproachability.

We say hi, then Phil strikes up a conversation with them about the upcoming Faux Mo gig. Phil has been single for the majority of the time I've known him, which is a long time. He's friendly and amiable.

The four of us chat and laugh comfortably, until another guy arrives and joins us, slipping an arm comfortably around Ellie's waist.

Right. So much for that idea.

Maddie is going out with one of Roger's work mates, it turns out.

Phil catches my disappointment and throws me a sly shrug.

Oh well.

Chapter 43

Later on Marco and I are sitting inside drinking shots of Agwa.

He asks if I've lost weight and I tell him a bit about what's been going on. I've known Marco since we were kids. He knows Claire, knows what she's like. Knows what I'm like.

I tell him about the day she dropped me on the side of the highway. I tell him that she said nobody would ever be interested in me. I tell him that I don't give a fuck what she thinks anymore, that I'm a free agent, that the relationship is pretty well over.

"Shit mate, that sucks. I'm sorry to hear it dude."

"Yeah."

We're pretty drunk, but it's still nice to have somebody on my side.

"You've gotta fuckin' do what's right for you though man. I couldn't be with someone who treated me like that. It's hard to watch sometimes."

"What do you mean?"

"We've all seen how she talks to you, mate. Remember when she threw that plate at you at Birdys? Or when you came to my birthday on the Coast and then had to drive back to Launceston because she thought Bec was sleazing on to you?"

"Bec was sleazing on to everybody."

"Exactly. What about the night you guys had that argument at that place in Queen Street and she pushed you off the balcony? That was fuckin scary!"

"I'd forgotten about that. Shit."

"It was *so* wrong. We were gonna say something then, probably should have. You'd be heaps better off by yourself mate, sorry to say it."

I nod. I don't want to get upset here, not in front of Marco, not in front of the party.

But he's probably right.

"The thing is, man, I *let* her do that all that stuff. I *let* her walk all over me. I could stop her, you know, I could leave at any time."

"You've got kids. And a house. It's not that simple and she knows it. You know it. But it'll all work itself out, you've just gotta take that first step and get out of there."

"I don't want to lose the girls."

"You won't. They'll always be your kids mate, Claire can't do anything about that."

"I don't want to fuck their lives up though either. My parents divorced when I was Little K's age and it was fucked. I still remember them fighting. I don't want my daughters to come from a broken home."

"You turned out all right though."

"Did I? Would we be having this conversation if I was all right?"

"You're not the problem, mate. I'm sorry to say it but you're not the problem. We all know it." He waves a hand at the backyard. "You know it. No one can do anything about it though. Except you."

"Thanks Marco."

"We'd fuckin have some fun if you were single mate. Happy to be your wingman anytime."

We clink our glasses together and drink. The Agwa is sweet and heady.

Chapter 44

TheUglyHusband: How's that sweet little booty of yours going? Keeping busy?

SecretChloe: Hey Hun, yeah my booty is getting plenty of action.

TheUglyHusband: On the beach? I'm looking for you every time I'm at any beach lol

SecretChloe: Yeah down to the beach and have stayed a couple of nights at guys houses. Ended up having a 3some the other night

TheUglyHusband: You have been busy... two guys?

SecretChloe: Yeah two guys, I've been with them before, so much fun

TheUglyHusband: Lol I bet.

SecretChloe: I'm am going to a wedding today too

TheUglyHusband: Ha ok. Got somebody lined up for the reception?

SecretChloe: Na but will just see who turn out

to be the horny uncle hahaha

Is she joking? I'm pretty sure she's joking.

TheUglyHusband: Bahaha oh dear.

SecretChloe: What have you got planned for this afternoon?

TheUglyHusband: heading to the beach for recovery time right now x

SecretChloe: cool. Keep an eye out for me down there lol xxx

Chapter 45

I t's good to have the girls home. I missed their little voices, the impromptu hugs, the bedtime stories.

It's not so great having Claire home.

We barely speak. Her eyes are slightly wider than usual, like she just saw a ghost. Or maybe like she's about to see one. Or make one.

I give her a wide berth and go about the business of checking my phone, working out, and checking my phone again.

The girls giggle the first few times they see me doing push-ups. Little K comes over to 'help' by sitting on my back and I make her stay there for three sets. My arms and shoulders burn. It feels great.

The sun is beating down on our backyard, so we spray each other with the garden hose and make plans to go to the beach as often as we can. I've never been that interested in going to beach... but

I am now.

I pull out our little barbeque and cook sausages for us all, shirt off, a Pure Blonde in one hand and a joint in the other. While I get pleasantly bombed and work on my tan, Claire dozes in the coolness of our bedroom. I leave her to it.

Despite the veneer of urban bliss, as the day goes on I become frustrated, restless. My holiday seems to be over.

I'm on *X* every five minutes. I make a fake *Facebook* profile and search around for local hookup groups, swinger groups, dogging groups... there are a few to join, but most of them haven't been updated in months.

By the time the girls go to bed the boredom is getting overwhelming. Claire is off in her own world, not avoiding me, but not engaging with me either. We've become used to doing our own things already.

Desperate for a bit of excitement, I finally hit up *Locanto* again. My email and accounts are anonymous, so I figure there's no harm in giving it a go.

I post an ad.

SNEAKING OUT: Married man seeking a horny woman for no strings attached fun in Hobart. One off or regular thing. I'm 35, tall, professional and well-mannered. You're younger than me, feminine and discreet. I love a dirty text or chat. I can come to you or meet somewhere public. 420 friendly.

And now I wait.

I'm not expecting any replies but having an open invitation out there in Internet land keeps me on the edge of my seat.

I do get a reply, only an hour later. It's a dude.

DUDE: Would you like some man on man? I'll get you there. I'm not gay, just curious.

I reply immediately.

TheUglyHusband: Nah sorry not my thing.

It's not my thing. I think back to the guy I saw in City Park.

Sure I've wondered what it would be like, skin on skin with another man... but nothing ever stirs. Not even a bit. I'm not gay, and I'm not curious.

I get a couple of other emails from bots – automated responses triggered by my ad. At first glance, the emails appear to be from real women until you see the web link at the bottom of their messages that says something like 'Click here to verify that you're a real person' or 'Click here to meet up with me in person'. Of course, clicking the link takes you to a new webpage designed to steal your soul (and your credit card details).

I wonder how many poor suckers have been ripped off by the fake responses to their *Locanto* ad. Because even though I know the emails are scams, even though I know they're not from a real person – and if one is from a real person, it's somebody far, far away who's probably desperate to get money out of me – there is still the inexplicable temptation to reply.

My brain wrestles with the distant possibility that there might actually be a horny local 21 year old with a generic *Hotmail* address that really wants to have a sexy chat on Skype.

I can understand why the loneliest people are the easiest targets for these scammers. I don't respond to any of them.

I give up and crawl into bed next to Claire.

She stirs, turns over, and puts her arms around me.

Chapter 46

My first day back at work.

There's nothing to do but stare at monitors and play with my phone.

SecretChloe posts just before lunchtime.

SecretChelsea: I'll be home soon, mum, just hanging out with a friend...

The post includes a .gif of a very naked young woman talking on her phone while being taken from behind by some anonymous dude.

She's so naughty.

I favourite the post, but I don't DM her about it. She knows I'm here.

Chapter 47

While I'm on the bus heading to work Miss_Innocent_Au posts a series of bathroom selfies that show her getting ready for the day.

The photos are rough, rushed - they don't do her any favours. Still the hyenas tell her how sexy she is, how she should show them more.

Miss_Innocent_Au: Be patient boys lol im at work x

Throughout the day she posts more selfies from her work bathroom, respectably bland.

Then at 4pm she posts again.

Miss_Innocent_Au: On my way home from work to an empty house. Pics soon!

The first photo, an hour later, gets the hyenas frothing.

Miss_Innocent_Au: Ready for some fun, boys?

She's wearing black lingerie – expensive black lingerie - and posing in an opulent hallway adorned with marble busts and vague oil paintings in gilded frames. She's styled, the room is remarkably well-lit, the lingerie brand new - it's a professional photo.

There's no way that photo could have been set up, taken and posted in under an hour.

None of her other followers question it. The photo is retweeted, favourited, discussed.

When I check in again later that night, Miss_Innocent_Au is fending off requests for more photos. She tells us she's watching a movie with her brother. She jokes that once the movie is over, she'll ask her brother to take a photo of her pussy.

Miss_Innocent_Au: He knows what his sister is like HAHAH!

The hyenas chortle digitally, slap their knees, congratulate her on her good humour, beg for a photo.

When the photo finally comes, it causes a small storm. It's her most explicit photo yet; her ass in the air, with a man's hand pulling her panties aside to reveal a very shapely pussy.

Miss_Innocent_Au: The money shot thanks little brother #MYBROTHERTOOKTHISPHOTOANDPULLEDMYUNDIESASIDEFORME

Wow.

The hyenas react immediately. There are quite a few predictable responses - "wow lucky brother" is the most common.

Sheesh. Do these guys drop out of school once they hit puberty, or are they actually typing with their dicks? It's hard to know.

There are a couple of WTF's too, but nowhere near as many as I might have thought.

Or as many as Miss_Innocent_Au was hoping for either, apparently; she retweets the photo again a short time later, with nothing but hash tags; #siblings #goodbrother #brothersisterlove #incest #keepitinthefamily

One of the hyenas buys in. He asks about her brother; older or younger? Have you ever done anything else with him?

Miss_Innocent_Au: I've always been comfortable being naked in front of my brother.

A few minutes later she posts 3 more photos. The same angle, the same ass, the same room.

The undies are gone and a huge, smooth dick is pushing inside her.

Miss_Innocent_Au: VERY COMFORTABLE LOL #ANYCOCKSACOCK

Almost immediately after the post, one of the hyenas replies.

BigBadBoner: Fake account everybody. It's a dude.

There is a link included in the reply.

I follow it to a Russian porn site featuring one

AnastasiaX. On the porn star's page is every photo Miss_Innocent_Au has posted so far.

BigBadBoner goes through and leaves the same reply on each one of her posts. This guy is really angry apparently

My own disappointment is relatively minor – this was all moving well beyond anything I'm interested in.

But the whole episode made me notice something. These guys - the hyenas - are completely invested in these X women. Even the men who never get a reply to their smooth salivating. They just keep trying.

It all seems so desperate, so seedy.

Am I becoming one of these guys too?

All of my interactions on here have been fun, respectful, but... once the novelty wears off, will I become one of them as well? Once the chatting stops being fun and becomes something else?

Chapter 48

Later, I'm on the verge of sleep when an unbidden thought strikes me cold.

What if SecretChloe is a fake?

What if she's not who she says she is?

I can't believe the idea hasn't occurred to be me before now.

For all I know, she could be a man in his fifties. It's not hard to find photos on the internet and pretend they're your own.

Laying there in bed next to Claire, in the middle of the night, I start to feel sick.

What if she's been playing me all along?

She could be a scammer.

She could be a guy who gets off on sexting other guys.

She could be some fucking vigilante group on a crusade to punish married men who go looking for random hook ups.

How would I know any different?

I feel sick, and foolish.

She's a random on the internet, of course she's fake. Of course she's too good to be real. Is any of it true? Are any of the photos real? Maybe she is who she says she is, but without the hook-ups and the gangbangs.

I don't know anything.

I can't sleep anymore. After an hour of trying to lie still, I get out of bed and sit in the lounge room with my laptop, going over our conversations.

Now there is a subtext to everything she has written. She doesn't talk about sex like any woman I've ever known.

She talks about sex like a man.

Like a hyena.

She talks about her ass a lot, about cocks and cum.

Maybe it's a guy who pretends to be a girl, or a dad pretending to be his daughter. Maybe it is a woman who has spent too much time looking at porn.

Was there ever an actual chance of hooking up with this person?

Is there any chance she is who she says she is?

I don't think so.

I feel so stupid.

I'm not angry at whoever it is. I'm angry at myself for being so gullible.

My body flushes with mortification as I remember the past few weeks, how turned on I had been by her messages, how the thought of possibly fucking her had helped propel me towards changing my life. I guess in that respect I should still be grateful.

It's tempting to message her, right now, and ask the question.

Instead, I go through the private photos she has sent me, save a few of them to my computer and open up Google's image search.

When I drop the photos into the search bar one by one, there are no results. That's a good sign – it means that Google hasn't been able to find the photos anywhere else on the internet.

She *could* be real. The glimmer of hope is thin, but I cling to it.

I watch the sun come up, depressed, unsure about the world, unsure about myself.

If I were to leave Claire after so many years of marriage, would I end up in this murky, anonymous world of pretend hook ups?

Instead of partying and travelling and meeting fun people, would I become another loser, sitting alone in the dark illuminated only by a screen, one hand on the mouse, the other on my dick, desperately waiting for some anonymous woman to acknowledge my filthy repartee?

Have I become one already?
This is the worst I've felt in weeks.

Chapter 49

I *am* losing weight. I can suddenly wear shirts that I haven't fit into in years.

It shouldn't be a surprise. Food has lost any appeal. I'm only eating once a day, usually at dinner with the family.

My new eating habits, combined with a fresh tan and a stringent exercise regime, mean that I'm looking better than I have in a very long time.

And I feel great. Only a month ago I was overweight, pasty, depressed and feeling utterly worthless.

Now I'm leaner, stronger and raring to go. It really does feel good.

I'm ravenously horny, from the moment I wake up to the moment I fall asleep.

Even though Claire only speaks to me in grunts and monosyllables, it's getting harder to keep my hands off her. Even with all the bullshit, the abuse, the manipulation, the cheating, it's hard to get past the fact that she's an extraordinarily attractive woman.

She's tanned and toned too - her summery body looks amazing.

I can't blame this Ronnie fucker for trying to snake his way in.

Then one night I'm lying on our bed in my underwear, watching her undress, watching her pull a sheer slip down over her near-naked body.

By the time she finishes, I'm rock hard.

She notices.

And she takes the slip off again.

The lamplight plays off her curves, making shadows across her caramel skin. Her breasts, softly taut, firmly round, take my breath away. Her delightfully stiff nipples make my lips tingle with desire.

For a few moments, we simply look at each other.

I'm not going to reach for her, despite my straining cock.

I'm *not.*

But I don't look away.

She kneels on the bed next to me, her breasts swaying hypnotically.

I *won't* reach for her.

She takes my underwear by the waistband and slowly pulls them down.

My stiff cock, bulging and sensitive, springs out. I lay very still, trying to control my breathing.

She lowers her head.

She licks my shaft from the bottom all the way to the tip, a slow, wet caress.

Her eyes are on mine as she takes me into her warm mouth.

I groan loudly.

For the first time in weeks – maybe months - my wife wants to fuck me.

Her tongue flicks along the underside of my shaft, her cheeks hollowing as she sucks me hard, tasting my skin, squeezing me with her lips.

She moves faster and I can't help but raise my hips, thrusting gently into her mouth.

Her soft whimper makes me thrust harder, and I wrap a hand up in her hair, holding her there. She closes her eyes, her breathing loud, her tongue lapping at my rock hard cock.

When she comes up for breath, she looks into my eyes again. Her naked desire makes my stomach flip. She takes me into her mouth again, eager, intent.

She moans hungrily and soon my cock is wet with her saliva and my precum. Her lips shine as she sits up, her hair falling across her face.

She's so fucking gorgeous. She climbs on top of me, straddles my cock, pushes herself against it, cries out when it spears into her tight, wet pussy.

She takes me all the way in and I groan at the way her soft flesh embraces my hardness.

And then she is thrusting, mindlessly driving herself onto my stiff rod, grinding against me, whimpering and moaning. I reach up and cup her bouncing breast, grazing her nipple with my thumb, and she throws her head back in abandon.

Her thighs begin to shake, an uncontrolled shuddering that spreads up her body and makes her whining louder and she is pumping faster and faster, rising my length, her juices running down my shaft as it slides in and out of her.

"Oh my...fucking... *god...*"

She tenses, her entire body stiffening, her gorgeous pussy glistening around my hard flesh... then she collapses onto me, gasping for breath, sweat beading on her forehead and across her chest.

A soft laugh pushes out of her lips relieved, almost disbelieving. She stays pressed against my chest for a few moments and I slowly slide my wet cock in and out of her.

Once she has caught her breath, I push her off me and onto her back.

She watches me get up and kneel between her thighs, her body spread open before me.

I guide my hard cock back inside her and she

groans again.

It's been a long time since our lovemaking was particularly eager… but I'm eager now.

Not for the gentle, considerate love-making that has been the mainstay of our sex life for so many years. No.

Nobody would ever want to fuck you.

There is no tenderness. I'm ruthless. I've been so horny for fucking weeks and the last woman I touched wasn't my wife.

I lift her hips off the bed and thrust into her, harder and harder.

I grind my cock against her, stretch her this way and that.

I hold her down, using her gorgeous body the way I want, pounding her mercilessly.

I fuck her until she's quivering, then I pull her onto all fours and push her head down onto her pillow.

I push deeper insider her, again and again, and she only stops shrieking when her voice gets hoarse and she closes her eyes as I drive my cock into her, over and over.

I take my time, putting her into the positions I want, fucking her the way that I want.

I only cum once I get tired.

And it takes a long time to get tired.

Chapter 50

C laire's cheerful this morning.

From the corner of my eye, I catch her looking at me appraisingly, with curiosity. For so long there has only been apathy or scorn in that gaze.

Instead of kissing her cheek as I leave to go to work, I bend her over our kitchen bench, lift up her dressing gown and spend a minute rubbing her pussy and her ass through her knickers.

She half-protests, grabbing my wrist feebly, but I push my fingers against her lips more and more firmly until I can feel dampness through her cotton panties.

Then I slap her ass and walk away, leaving her bent over and gasping, her dressing gown up around her waist, her hair in her face, her eyes bulging.

I'm hard for the entire bus ride to work.

Chapter 51

I'm feeling good.

And I have plans.

Faux Mo.

Faux Mo is an annual festival organised by the Museum of Old and New Art, Hobart's cultural gatekeeper. While the festival itself consists of a few dozen events across a range of venues, it is the afterparty that's the festival's hottest ticket.

Given my new outlook - and the fact that it's likely to be my only proper night out this summer - I'm determined to make the most of it.

Tonight, I will play.

It's the first real opportunity to test out my new approach to the universe.

In years past, the afterparty has featured models (naked) suspended in a cage high above the audience, a DJ in a broom closet with room for one dancer, a man painted entirely gold serving absinthe from a glass stiletto, a grotesquely overweight MC (again, naked) rapping to a huge crowd, a refurbished bus where each seat has a pipe mouthpiece connected to a huge central Hookah, a monstrous pipe organ that filled the air with fire and industrial groans, a powerful spotlight array that beamed light high into the clouds above the city, an air balloon shaped like a mutated sea cow, a troupe of dancers (nakedest) offering free hugs to VIP ticket holders... it's a big old party for little old Hobart.

I head down to the Republic Bar to meet some mates for preloads.

The place is packed. Jason has a table outside in the beer garden so I join him. Paul, Tonga, Tim and Tim's girlfriend are already there.

I haven't seen Tim in years. His girlfriend, almost a decade younger than him, pouts at us all, bored. We ignore her and catch up over a few pints.

It's good chats, but time passes quickly and before we know it, it's time to head to Faux Mo.

In my efforts to shrug off the general shyness towards women I've developed over the course of my relationship with Claire, I decide to smile back at any woman who smiles at me.

It probably sounds easy. It's not. I'm so used to dropping my eyes.

Luckily enough I get a chance to practice before

we even get into the place. As we finally reach the head of the queue into the main entrance, I notice three women walking past, looking for the end of the line.

One of them catches my eye and flashes me a smoky smile. I hold her eyes and smile back. She doesn't break the eye contact until one of her friends pulls here away.

"I saw that." Jason laughs and elbows me. "She one of Claire's friends?"

"I fucking hope not."

This year, the after party is being held in a dilapidated government building, just off the waterfront. The site itself is slated for demolition - this time next year, this huge old four-storey building will be a cold empty plaza. MONA, in its usual unimpeachable style, has 'activated' the space for the after party.

'Activating a space' apparently means sticking a bar on every floor, a DJ in every room and getting some college-level art students to decorate with stuff their mum bought from The Reject Shop. Every room leads to another room and every corner reveals another crowd. It's dark, it's dinghy and purposefully seedy.

I love it.

Not long after we get inside, Tim and his girlfriend start arguing. She wants to leave. He doesn't.

After the past couple of months the last thing I want to do is to watch a couple fight, so I ditch them.

This is *my* night.

Chapter 52

There are six or seven dance floors to choose from. The big one outside is packed, with most of the crowd squashing up to the front to get closer to the DJ, which in turn prevents anyone from actually dancing. Fucking dolts.

The DJ on the third floor is mixing some hard trance - perfect.

I buy a couple of drinks, take off my jacket, and pull up some floor.

I love dancing. I always have. A lot of my mates refuse to dance - they don't know what they're missing.

However, it doesn't take long to discover that I'm nowhere near as fit as I thought. After ten minutes, I'm sweating buckets. It's hard to tell if people are moving away from me on the dancefloor or if I'm just imagining it.

The cold beer helps, but only momentarily. My shirt is soaked. Sweat is running down my face and back in rivulets. The other people on the dancefloor look cool and collected, but if I keep this up I'm going to stink for the rest of the night.

It's a wakeup call. I've still got a long way to go to get in to shape.

I head outside for some fresh air. The outdoor stage is still packed, but after a minute or two I find Jason nestled away in a corner of the courtyard, just underneath a steel external staircase.

It's an awkward spot, but there's space for three or four people to actually sit down so I park myself next to him.

"Nice find."

"Well, yeah," he stretches. "Fuck standing up all night. Plus…"

He nods towards the staircase. I follow his eye line… and immediately look away.

The stairs are packed as people slowly make their way from the outside area to the room on the third floor - and from where Jason and I are sitting you can see up the skirt of every woman who is wearing one.

"Worth the forty bucks to get in," Jason sniggers.

Three girls, all wearing tiny skirts, are climbing the stairs. Two of them are wearing G-strings.

The view is fantastic… but it makes me feel like a pervert.

Like a hyena.

Jason stinks of desperation. He's not even trying to talk to any of the girls going past. He's content to lean back and watch their asses wriggle by, like a schoolboy under the bleachers.

As attractive as all the summery legs and tiny panties are, I just can't stay here. It's too creepy for me. I feel like a desperate old man, a voyeur in the corner, a starving hyena drooling over skin I'll never get to taste.

Besides, a few people are noticing us and shaking their heads in disgust - it's pretty obvious what is going on.

I punch Jason in the arm.

"Gotta wander. Coming for a sticky beak?"

Jason looks at me as if he can't believe what he's hearing.

"Ah... no," he chortles, shaking his head, eyeing me like I'm crazy. "This is the best show in town, I'm not going fuckin anywhere!"

"Righto. I'll be back."

I groove through the crowd and climb the stairs I've just been sitting under.

When I'm half way up, I stop and shake my ass ostentatiously. I look down at Jason; he's laughing, covering his eyes.

There are two girls watching me. They follow my gaze down to see Jason under the stairs and their faces crinkle in disgust. One gives me the evil eye, but I shrug and go on my way.

Chapter 53

One dancefloor, two dancefloors, three dancefloors, four.

I drink at the bars and smoke joints in the courtyards. There's a DJ around every corner. I drift through the whole venue, looking for my groove.

Eventually I find it in the basement.

The room is tiny, dark and concrete, with glow-in-the-dark paint spattered around the industrial walls. The DJ booth is set up on a scaffold high above the floor. People are dancing with their heads down, working it, not dancing to be looked at or to look at anyone else, but simply to get lost in the music.

Sometime later, I stagger out of the little room. I'm drenched with sweat and I stink, but I don't care anymore.

As I'm threading through the crowd, I notice another small doorway on the basement level and head for it, hoping there might be a pop-up bar on the other side.

There's no bar. It's a small chill out room decorated like a jungle, with ragged palms lilting around the walls and large cushions strewn around the floor.

I don't see anybody that I recognise, but there is a group of blokes standing up to leave, shrugging into their leather jackets and flexing their muscles at each other. Once they vacate, I pull over one of the cushions they were using and flop into it.

I've been sitting there for maybe a minute when my hand brushes something buried in the folds of the cushion - a small plastic bag. A scambag.

I quickly shove it into my pocket, catching a glimpse of white powder in the process.

This could turn into a very interesting night.

Chapter 54

I'm trying to resist pulling the scambag out again for a closer look when the woman who smiled at me in the queue breezes into the room with her friends. They claim a trio of cushions in the corner and settle in, waving their champagne flutes like sceptres.

She spots me pretty quickly and smiles. I smile back, regretting the sweaty dampness of my back.

She climbs over the cushions between us.

"Hey," she greets me like an old friend.

"Hey there," I reply, trying not to stink. "I was hoping I'd run into you."

She likes that.

"Why are you sitting here by yourself?"

"The fellas are dancing," I lie. "I just wanted to chill for a minute. I'm glad I did, now."

"Me too."

It isn't long before I make a move. She's a great kisser and it's pretty clear from the get go what she's looking for.

After a few minutes her friends get up and leave us to our making out. Nobody else in the dark little room is paying any attention to us.

I'm about to pull her on to my lap when two big guys come into the room.

Come *back* into the room - it's two of the blokes who were leaving when I first came in. One of them looks really nervous. The other is furious. They ignore us and start picking up cushions, turning them over, shaking them out, looking for something.

Instead of pulling her onto my lap, I kiss her lightly and then pull away.

"I need to use the bathroom." I whisper to her, feeling slightly ridiculous. You just can't make something like that sound sexy. "Will you wait for me?"

She nods. We kiss lightly again.

My legs feel like they've got no strength left but I manage to step over the people laying on the other cushions and past the two increasingly stressed heavies. Back into the Faux Mo maelstrom. There is a toilet nearby and I head straight for it.

The queue is short and lively with the usual drunken back-slapping and boofhead cat-calling that goes on in male toilets at any busy music festival. After a couple of minutes I've got a cubicle to myself. I shut the door, lock it, and turn my back to it.

The little scambag is full of white powder. Full almost to bursting. The powder is mostly fine, almost oily, with a few larger pebbles spread through it.

I think I know what it is, so I open it up, dip my little finger in and have a taste. Just like a cop in an '80s TV show.

I recognise that sharp, metallic taste immediately, even though it's been years. My tongue and lips are numb.

Cocaine.

I look at the bag more closely.

The last time I had cocaine, I threw in fifty dollars for a $300 gram that was shared by maybe eight people over the course of a night. I had three lines from that gram and it was plenty enough for me.

There is more than a gram in this scambag. A hell of a lot more.

I'm looking at over a grand's worth of coke, at the very least.

And it's good. Even after the little taste I had, I can feel my body filling with energy, with false adrenaline.

I scoop some more out with the back of my fingernail and snort it.

My blood tingles.

I'm ready to dance again.

Which reminds me of the girl - the sexy girl I was kissing just minutes ago, who is still waiting for me in the chill out, probably wondering where the fuck I am.

I carefully seal the scam bag, close it in my wallet, and head back to the chill out room.

The girl is still there on the cushion waiting, playing on her phone. She looks up at me and her smile makes my stomach flip.

The two heavies are still there too. They're talking to a young guy, a skinny raver who is clearly shitting himself. The raver's friends are sitting behind him, eyeing each other nervously. The heavies look pretty fired up.

As I watch, one of the heavies makes the raver lift his arms above his head; the other heavy starts to pat him down, searching.

Oh shit.

My wallet feels like it's burning a hole in my back pocket. My heart pounds. I look from the heavies to the girl waiting, to the heavies again... then I hold my hand out to the girl.

She doesn't hesitate to take it, and when I pull her to her feet she laughs and stumbles.

"What are you..."

"Come on!"

I turn around to lead her out… and walk straight into the other two heavies, nearly knocking one of them over. He zeroes in on me immediately.

"Oy! Fucking slow down!" He straightens up his jacket, glaring at me.

"Sorry man," I offer, hoping he won't see how high I suddenly feel. "Didn't see you there."

The other guy is peering into the chill out room, looking for his mates. He calls to them. "Have you found it?" I don't hear a response.

"What's the hurry?" The heavy demands, standing toe to toe with me. He's trying to intimidate me, but I'm bulletproof.

Feeling ten feet tall, I nod at the gorgeous girl holding my hand.

"What do you fuckin reckon?"

He hesitates and we glide past him without waiting for an answer, I quickly lead her towards the stairwell.

"*Oy!*" He calls after us. "Come back here!"

The other heavy sticks his head out of the door to the chill out. "Come and help us fuckin' *look,* Paddy!"

I stop at the bottom of the staircase and look back - Paddy is still watching us, his brow furrowed. He looks into the room then, back at me.

I resist the temptation to smirk at him as we hightail it up the stairs.

He doesn't follow.

Chapter 55

The top floor of the building is less populated and the dancefloor is almost empty. Hallways shoot off in odd directions and lead to small, strange rooms washed in Faux Mo's trademarked red light.

In one room, a rapturous crowd watches a scantily dressed woman plays barrelhouse piano while a scantily dressed man paints a wall using a broomstick strapped to his groin.

In another, there is an old projector playing gay pornography from the 1970s while a dozen people loll around on filthy couches.

In the next, there is a small cocktail bar, filled to the brim with laughing hipsters.

The next room we find has a thin rope across the entrance. It's a small bathroom, glowing with brilliant red light. I can see a bathtub where a mannequin's head is partially submerged in dark water alongside an old-fashioned radio. An exhibition, of sorts.

I step over the rope and hold her hand as she follows.

Behind the open door, out of sight, is an old vanity unit with a cracked mirror and a dusty sink.

Her arms wrap around my shoulders as we kiss and my hands find her firm ass. She pushes against me, her mouth insistent, her hips rocking back and forth against my bulging groin.

I turn her around and lift her up onto the old vanity. It rocks a little as she lifts her legs to wrap around my waist, her skirt riding up, her panties warm against my skin.

Her heavy breath is filling my mouth, her hands grabbing at my shoulders, my back, my butt, pulling me closer, making me grind against her.

As she pulls back for air, the red light makes shadows across her gorgeous face. Her eyes are dark and hungry.

"*Fuck* me," she demands, and kisses me again. "Fuck me *right* now."

Without a word I unzip and pull my hard cock out, nudging it against her thin cotton panties, gasping at the plump softness beneath. She moans, gripping my shoulders and lifting her knees even higher as I drag the head of my cock over her warm mound.

I kiss her deeply again, tasting her coppery

tongue as she shifts her shoulders. Suddenly her cool fingers are tickling my cock while she pulls her panties to the side.

She wraps her hand around my thickness and guides me forward.

Her wet pussy deliciously parts around my cock and we both groan as I push inside her.

She grips my hair, raises her knees to let me get deeper and I slowly ease all the way to the hilt. Her tongue flickers desperately in my mouth and she hums as I pull back, then groans again as I thrust forward.

She is marvellously tight. Every movement send a spark of electricity through my body.

I put my hand around her hips, where her skirt has ridden up and hold her tight, fucking her faster, thumping against the vanity unit. She rocks back and forth, moaning around my tongue, her juices making us both wet.

I bounce on my toes, driving into her. Her face is a hungry smirk, her lips quivering, her eyes bright, her skin glowing red.

"Harder," she rasps. "Fucking *harder."*

I pound into her, fucking her wet cunt with long, hard strokes that make her growl.

Pulling down the front of her blouse reveals a lacy black bra that folds away to reveal a delight-fully small, hard nipple. I lower my lips to it, my hips thrusting, and she squeals as I flick it with my tongue.

Her nipple tastes delightful, her small, firm breast rising into my mouth.

After a moment she grunts and pushes my head away. Her teeth are clenched, her eyes wild.

She grips my wrist and lifts my hand to her throat.

"Choke me," She pants. "Fucking *hurt* me."

Electricity surges through my cock and for a moment I can only gasp at her.

She squeezes my hand, her eyes fixed on mine.

"*Do it*, fucking cho…"

I tighten my grip around her throat and her eyes roll back in her head. Her body stops moving and her mouth hangs open. I slowly pull back, almost withdraw, then *plunge* into her again, hard and rough.

Her body shudders.

I do it again, and again, shoving my cock into her mercilessly, watching her gorgeous face struggle for breath. Her cunt tightens around me and I force myself deep inside her, grinding against her.

When I let go of her throat, she gasps a deep breath and whines piteously.

I slap her gorgeous face.

She looks up at me, gasping for breath, hair in her eyes, a disbelieving smile curling the corners of her mouth.

I slap her again and she shrieks, wrapping her legs around me, pulling my cock deep inside.

I grip her throat again and shove my tongue into her gaping mouth, my hard cock fucking piercing into her.

Suddenly she's shaking, her body thrumming against mine, and I squeeze her neck and plunge into her shivering cunt, feeling her lift off the vanity, her hips rocking against mine as she cums with a loud, desperate shriek that fills my ears and makes my blood boil.

Her entire body is slamming down on my cock, over and over, as I hold her in the air by her neck, slapping her bouncing ass with my free hand, thrusting my tongue into her gaping, gasping mouth…

I lift onto my toes as a spine-tingling orgasm surges through my body and into hers.

My grip tightens on her throat as I grind her softening body onto my spasming cock. Heat radiates from her scarlet face and I lick her lips as my cum drains into her in streams.

When I let go, she gasps a deep breath and lets out a low, animalistic moan and I gently lower her back onto the vanity. She leans back and I withdraw, my wet cock springing out of her, leaving a trail of thick white cum that drips out of her.

Her pussy is neatly shaven, a gorgeous mess of sweat and cum. Without thinking, I reach down and gently push my sticky load back inside of her with a fingertip.

She gasps again, her eyes opening, fixing on mine.

Without looking away, I lift my sticky fingers to her lips and she slowly cleans them with her tongue.

My cock twitches again.

I'm about to lift her knees back up when there is a commotion in the doorway.

"What the *fuck?*"

It is a small, stocky woman wearing all black and a bright red lanyard. She looks pissed off.

"You can't *be* in here, you have to… what are you *doing?*"

I quickly pack my cock away as the girl slides off the vanity, pulling down her skirt.

"Sorry," I say to the security guard. "We were just…"

"Get out." Her voice is stern, no nonsense. "Now. This is an *exhibition.*"

I can't help but smirk as I look around the dinghy, red-lit bathroom.

"Is it? I mean, we thought…"

"Out! *Now!*"

Ducking my head, I lead the girl out of the bathroom. She's still straightening herself up, adjusting her skirt, combing her hair with her fingers. The security guard watches us go with a scowl.

A few steps down the hallway, I turn to lead us into the tiny cocktail bar but the girl lets go of my hand.

She leans in to kiss my cheek, then whispers in my ear.

"I wish my husband would fuck me like that."

Before I can say anything, she's walking off.

Mouth hanging open, I watch her cute ass wiggle its way into the crowd. There are stains on the bottom of her skirt. My stains.

And then she's gone.

I realise that I never asked her name. She didn't ask mine, either.

The security guard walks past the doorway where I'm standing and scowls again, shaking her head.

Snorting laughter, I sidle over to the bar and order a cocktail.

I'm so goddamned thirsty.

Chapter 56

After a fruitless search for Tim and the others, I bail. Faux Mo is huge and the chances of the heavies finding me again – or even recognising me - is pretty slim, but I'm still not willing to risk it. Its after 2am now anyway so the party will shut down soon.

It's too early to go home, so I head to a nearby club - the Pooh Bar. It's quiet, but I don't mind.

I order a bourbon on the rocks and take it into the club's bathroom.

Another short sniff of the white powder. This stuff is great.

For the next hour or so, I dance.

I don't care about my sweat, or my stink, or girls or any of it. Just the music.

For a while I've got the dancefloor to myself but just after three, when Faux Mo closes, the crowd starts drifting in. The dancefloor fills up, so I get another bourbon and retire to a leather armchair to rest and watch.

The DJ ramps it up, mixing some swing classics from the '40s with some tight breakbeats. It's good. The kids like it.

Leaning back in the leather chair, bourbon in my hand and cocaine in my blood, I'm the coolest I've ever been. I own the entire city.

When one girl on the dancefloor turns towards me and watches me watching her, I feel like some kind of gangster king.

She glides her hips from side to side, smooths her long light skirt over her lower belly, holds my gaze, steps closer. Neither of us smile.

I'm about to uncross my legs and invite her on to my royal knee when a hand grabs her elbow.

Some young guy's drunken face appears over her shoulder and speaks into her ear. She nods, then follows him off the dancefloor, not even glancing back at me.

Maybe I imagined the whole thing.

I watch them go, cool as a fucking cucumber.

It doesn't bother me. Nothing bothers me.

Nothing will ever bother me again.

Chapter 57

I try and stay away from *X*, but it keeps drawing me back.

SecretChloe keeps drawing me back.

While it was kind of a delicious tease, sexting with this anonymous young lady, the idea of it has now become a kind of torture.

I don't even know if she's a woman. I don't know what to think.

Her photos must be real, I tell myself. They're not showing up anywhere else on the net, which means she must have posted them herself.

But is it actually SecretChloe in the photos? There's only one way to know for sure.

If she's not real, then I've been making a fool of myself for weeks anyway… what harm is there in drawing it out a little longer?

TheUglyHusband: I want to fuck you tonight

I get on with my day and try not to think about those powder blue panties.

SecretChloe: I need your cock so bad.

TheUglyHusband: Let me give it to you.

There is a long pause before her next message.

SecretChloe: Can you come over later? Around ten?

I rub my eyes and read it again. Butterflies tickle my stomach.

The next message is an address on Hobart's Eastern Shore.

I gape at my phone. Sweat is beading on my chest. My hands are shaking and so is the phone. It takes me way longer than it should to respond.

TheUglyHusband: I'll be there x

SecretChloe: Good. Don't knock on the door, just msg when you get here.

TheUglyHusband: Done.

Holy fuck.

My head is spinning.

Chapter 58

The evening passes in a blur. I float through my chores, float out into my car and float across the Tasman Bridge. None of it seems real.

I can't remember where I told Claire I was going.

I park down SecretChloe's street.

It's a quiet suburban night time scene - green lawns, creeping cats, a TV glowing in every third house.

Like a thief in the night, I shuffle up to the address she gave me.

The house is big. There are lights on at either end of the building, two cars parked in the drive-way, garden gnomes nestled happily in the garden.

I walk across the street to stand in the shadows and msg her.

TheUglyHusband: I'm here.

For almost a minute there is no response and I bounce nervously from foot to foot.

Then...

SecretChloe: Go up the path to the side of the house and wait. Be quiet pls x

I do it.

The pathway leads away from the front door, into the shadows on the far side of the house. I tiptoe past a large, curtained window that hums a faint hip-hop beat, and duck around the corner to the side of the house.

There is the door.

My hands are trembling. I try to control my breathing.

What the fuck am I *doing* here?

Abruptly I'm hit with a tide of doubt.

This has to be a catfish, a setup, a scam. When the door opens, it'll be an old man.

Or a group of men with blunt weapons.

Or the police.

I almost bolt.

Almost.

Then the door opens.

It's not an old man, but I couldn't have been more shocked if it was.

The girl that emerges is gorgeous.

Not just *pretty*, not just *attractive* - she looks like an American Apparel model in her loose white t-shirt and tight blue jeans. Her dark hair is long and artfully wavy, falling around her slender shoulders.

And she's young. Far younger than I was expecting. If she's twenty years old, then I'm Kurt Cobain.

I stare at her, stunned. This *can't* be SecretChloe. I must have woken up her sister.

I brace myself for the startled scream, but it never comes.

The girl spots me and steps over lightly, looking me up and down. Even in the dark, I can see that she's grinning.

Before I can speak she stretches onto her toes, kisses me lightly on the lips and then quickly steps away.

"You can't come in, dad's on the computer in the next room. Wait here."

She disappears inside again. I'm left gaping at the door.

That *was* Chloe? What the fuck is going on? Her dad?

Am I being set up? Why did she tell me to...

The door opens again and my mind goes blank.

She's still wearing the white t-shirt, but the jeans are gone. Black panties peek from under the hem of her t-shirt.

She kisses me again - not lightly this time. Her tongue is cool and firm, hungry.

She breaks the kiss off before I can even lift my hands. I'm stunned to the point of paralysis, even as she kneels down and unzips me.

I still haven't even spoken to her... and she's putting my cock in her mouth.

I'm rock hard in moments as she works me with her hand and tongue, her eyes smiling up at me. Her other hand sneaks down into her black panties.

I stifle my groans as she licks the head, then takes the whole thing deep into her mouth.

Her hands pull my hips forward, trying to push me in further. I can't control my gasp when her tongue sneaks out to tickle my balls.

Abruptly she pulls her face away, but her hand keeps working as she stands up and kisses me again.

Now her lips are warm.

She pulls away, smiling at me, biting her bottom lip, her hand squeezing my shaft. Without losing her grip, she turns around. I hadn't even noticed her taking her panties off.

She pushes her naked ass towards me, gripping my cock in her hand.

My knob slides over her wetness, twice, three times... and then I'm inside her. She pushes again and I slide all the way in, rock hard against her soft, warm flesh.

Her pussy is delicious. My toes curl as her tightness wraps around me, lets me go, then draws me in again.

She pushes so hard that I'm almost knocked off balance, so I take her by the hips, spread my feet, and give it to her.

Her gasps are stifled, but she bites her lip and pulls me deeper.

I run my hand over the small of her back. Her skin is tanned and firm, flawless.

Her warmth squeezes every nerve in my cock and before long I feel my balls shifting, ready to explode.

She feels it too.

Without missing a beat, she wraps a hand around the base of my shaft and lifts herself off it. Then she slowly licks her fingertips and wipes slick wetness onto the head of my cock.

"I want your cum in my ass," she insists, breathless.

My expression makes her giggle.

My cock is already bulging as she pushes it against her other hole.

Her breathing grows even more ragged.

"Just the tip, just the tip… *oh...*"

The tip squeezes in, slowly.

My brain is melting. Her tight ass closes around the rim of my knob and she sighs happily.

She pulls away and it pops out.

I've never been so hard in my life.

She pushes against me, more slowly this time, and my cock pulses as it slips into her ass.

"Give it to me, fucking give it to me!"

Her hand squeezes my shaft, my balls, and then my shaft again as her ass closes around my knob.

I want to push it into her, to cum deep inside her, but it feels far too tight.

She eases back and her tightness squeezes unbearably around my cock… and then I'm coming, coming uncontrollably, coming straight into her ass.

She throws her head back and moans as I empty my balls into her. She squirms and wriggles, pulling my cock around with her body, drawing out every last drop.

My brain is collapsing.

After a few moments, she lifts away again and I fall out of her, another bead of cum blooming on my knob.

Looking back at me, breathing hard and fast, she touches her ass and sighs at the white droplets on her fingertips.

I back away and look at her, my cock waving through the air like a descending crane. She straightens up and pulls her panties back on.

I'm still catching my breath when she stands on her tiptoes and gives me a light, chaste kiss on the lips.

Her eyes are laughing.

"Next time we'll have longer."

She smiles broadly at me, then steps away.

The door swings open and closed and she is gone.

I'm standing in a random backyard in the dark, my drooping dick sticky and slick, my heart pumping adrenaline, my mind racing.

Then I hear a noise from inside the house - a door closing - and it gets me moving.

I'm driving back across the bridge before the adrenaline fades away and it all hits me.

I start laughing and crank the stereo as loud as it will go.

Nobody would ever want to fuck you.

Wrong, baby.

And just like that, I'm on top of the fucking world.

Chapter 59

We're lying in bed, our sweat drying on the sheet, trying to catch our breath.

Claire's distracted. There's something on her mind.

She tells me that something happened while she was dropping the girls at school this morning. She was getting them out of the car, sorting out bags and books and lunchboxes, when a bashed up Jeep drove past.

The Jeep was full of people, the passenger side window was down, and a toothless scumbag in the passenger seat had leered at her.

Focused on herding the girls towards school, she hadn't paid the bogans any attention… until one of them shouted at the top of his lungs.

"Oi! You like *cock?* Me mate 'ere wants ta *fuck yer in yer arse!"*

She could hear the other men in the car laughing as they zoomed off.

She explains to me that it wasn't what he shouted, or the fact that he was in a car full of men, that upset her.

"That's normal," she shrugs. "You get used to that as a teenager. But it was eight thirty in the morning. Outside a school. The girls were standing right there with me and there were other kids and parents everywhere... and I felt like I had done something wrong. Like it was *my* fault that these... these *fuckheads*... decided to shout about my ass in front of all these people."

She's angry. And so she should be. I'm angry too.

There's something about the way an attractive woman makes you feel. I don't think it's the same for a woman who is seeing an attractive man... I might be wrong, how the fuck should I know.

But for men - no for *me* - it actually provokes a physiological response. I'm not talking about my cock. I mean it literally causes a physical shock. If I see a stunning woman, my chest lurches, my stomach flips and my head gets light.

It's not a good thing – we've been told again and again that women shouldn't be objectified, shouldn't be reduced to simple physical beings, shouldn't be unwittingly sexualised.

I know this stuff. I know it well. But knowing doesn't help.

If I see a woman I'm attracted to, then I'm attracted to her. My body reacts before my mind can censure it. Even though it's wrong, even though it makes me a schmuck to be attracted to a person I don't even know, I just can't help it.

I love the way that seeing an attractive woman makes me feel, but I don't shout at them about my dick because I'm not a fucking animal.

I'm not a hyena.

I'm *definitely* not a hyena.

Chapter 60

S ecretChloe posts a photo of her pussy first thing in the morning.

It's divine. Her soft, smooth flesh is something sublime, something to murder for, something to start a war over.

It's hard to believe that I've touched such flaw-less skin, have plundered it with my own rude flesh. I could look at it all day.

SecretChloe: Has your wife been working your dick?

TheUglyHusband: She has been working it hard. Sometimes I think about your little pussy when I'm deep inside her

SecretChloe: Does it make your cock harder and make you fuck her harder when you think about me

TheUglyHusband: It makes my cock so stiff and I fucking pound her with it. When I'm close to cumming I think about squeezing my cock into your little ass and exploding

SecretChloe: that was so much fun! More please x

I've spent a few hours now reading through Claire's *Facebook* messages, searching for any more clues that she's cheating. There are conversations that are years old; every conversation she's had since she first joined *Facebook* seven or eight years ago.

I only glance at most of them. Some I read more carefully; the conversations with guys I don't know, the ones with guys I do know… and don't trust.

There aren't many of either.

Only a couple of guys have directly asked her out via *Facebook* and she shut them both down immediately. One or two longer conversations turn a little flirty but end soon afterwards.

I can't tell if she's deleted the more incriminating conversations and messages, or if she had those conversations using other messaging software, or if they were never there at all – but there's nothing here that suggests she actually hooked up with someone else.

I'm relieved of course… but there's no way of knowing whether I'm getting the whole story.

Then I see my name mentioned a couple of times in a more recent conversation. I decide to read it; Christ knows I'm not getting anything from Claire herself.

Claire: We had the worst fight ever on Christmas Day in front of my whole family. He told me that he doesnt care, that I don't get to tell him what to do anymore. He said he would leave me and take the girls.

Ashley: Oh babe are you ok?

Claire: I dont know. I dont know anything.

Ashley: You two will work it out. Youve been together forever.

Claire: i dont know. It was different this time. I've never seen him like that before. Like he could just walk away.

Ashley: he loves you. And the girls too.

Claire: He was so angry. He said he wouldnt be taken for granted any more.

Ashley: You dont take him for granted babe he's lucky to have you.

Claire: no i do though. I thought he needed me more than I needed him. He showed me that wasn't true. I've driven him away.

Ashley: You've been frustrated with him for ages so its hard when the power shifts but yeah maybe you have to go along with it for a while.

Claire: yeah i guess so. Just dont know if it will make any difference now.

Ashley: he loves you

Claire: i dont know if he does. I dont know anything

Ashley: oh Clairebear xxx

I never thought about the change in our relationship in those sort of terms – as a power shift I mean. I guess I never really thought about relationships in that way.

But the more I think about it, the more sense it makes.

First she had the power over the relationship, over me. She called the shots. She did whatever she wanted. It was always me backing down and making sure that we stayed together.

Now *I* don't give a fuck… and apparently the power has shifted to me?

I'm not calling the shots, but I am doing whatever I want. And it feels like a weight has been lifted off me.

For the first time in years, I'm starting to feel like myself again.

Chapter 61

When I wake up there are two messages from SecretChloe. The first was sent just after 4am.

SecretChloe: I have just been woken up by a heap of texts from a guy in his 60's wanting to fuck me.

And then, an hour later...

SecretChloe: Fucked him on my neighbour's lawn lol back in bed now x

I reply while I'm drinking my morning coffee. Claire is buzzing around in the kitchen, trying to get ready for work.

TheUglyHusband: Wow really, you took a 4am booty call? That's wicked. Would love to know the story of how you started fucking a guy in his 60s

I get dressed for work, kiss the girls goodbye and hit the bus.

It's almost lunchtime when the next message

comes in.

SecretChloe: Oh yeah he is a great fuck! Just a random meet one day, swapped numbers, went from there

TheUglyHusband: Wow he must be smooth, I'm impressed lol i hope I'm fucking girls like you in my 60's

SecretChloe: he loves my ass, thinks it's the greatest thing in the world lol

TheUglyHusband: It is. Does he eat it for you?

SecretChloe: Oh yeah, that's a must. He goes straight for it, makes me bend over doggy for him to eat it

TheUglyHusband: Oh man I would love to put you on all fours, pull your panties down and open you up with my tongue. Do you like his tongue in ur ass?

SecretChloe: I fucking love it, drives me wild. Makes my pussy drip too.

TheUglyHusband: Both your holes need fucking after that then

SecretChloe: Of course they do lol he came in my ass this morning too, just like you did. When i got up again i had breakfast with mum and i was laughing to myself about how like two hours ago i had a cock in my butt and now I'm sitting with my mum lol

TheUglyHusband: Wow, you're so naughty,

she has no idea?

SecretChloe: Nah no idea at all. I have been getting fucked in the sand dunes before and mum and dad have walked past along the beach lol

Now that I have a face and a body to put to her stories, they're so much easier to visualise. It strikes me that I should probably be jealous; but I'm not.

I like thinking about her getting off.

TheUglyHusband: Lololol no way that's hilarious! Their little angel. Have you fucked any of your dad's friends?

SecretChloe: True! Yeah two of his mates and about a week after I fucked them he invited them and a few others around to watch the football and a bbq

TheUglyHusband: I bet they weren't interested in the football lol.

Chapter 62

Later, Claire goes out with her girlfriends. I'm at home edging - watching porn and reading back over today's conversation with SecretChloe - waiting for her to come home. If she doesn't get home before I go to bed, I'll sort myself out.

But I'd rather she came home.

When she does get home, just after eleven, she's pretty drunk. I've been keeping an eye on her *Facebook* messages, even though I tell myself that I don't care what she does anymore. I know that she's been having a good time.

But she's in an awful mood.

After a bit of digging, she explains that she had run into Anica, Marco's recently dropped ex-girlfriend. Anica, still bitter over the end of her relationship, apparently told Claire everything I had drunkenly told Marco at Roger's party few weeks back - how our relationship was over, how

I was just waiting for the right time to leave.

Fucking Marco. Thanks, champ.

We sit outside under the stars, each of us with a joint in our hand.

She asks me if it is true.

"It was true, then."

"And now?"

I don't know what to say, so I don't say anything.

I should tell her about Lisa. I should ask her about Ronnie. I should tell her about SecretChloe... but all I care about, right now, is fucking her.

When she goes to bed half an hour later, I follow.

She lays with her back to me, cold and un-friendly. I run my hand up her back and over her hips. She shifts and stretches, so I pull her close.

I eat her pussy until she cums. Then she rides me until she cums again.

Then, finally, it's my turn.

Chapter 63

The next day, we're sitting in the garden in the sunshine. The girls are inside watching Netflix.

Claire's telling me some innocuous story from the night before when I reach over and put my hand up her skirt.

She breaks off the telling as I stroke her pussy through her white panties.

Her eyes flick to the front gate - anybody walking past could see us - but she doesn't flinch when I stand up and pull out my hard cock. She goes to work.

I fuck her in the sunshine, on our outdoor setting. She doesn't bother to lower her voice and by the time she cums she is shrieking at the top of her lungs. I pull out and spray her.

While she goes inside to clean up, I roll a joint and smoke it under the tree, still naked. It feels great.

When my phone buzzes, I don't rush to pick it up.

SecretChloe: Been getting any?

TheUglyHusband: Yeah I just came lol

I'm still pretty hard, sitting naked in the sunshine, so I take a quick photo of my junk and send it to her.

TheUglyHusband: Still wet from her x

SecretChloe: Ohhhnice, did you cum inside her or just over her?

TheUglyHusband: All over her. Like... All over her lol

SecretChloe: mmm jealous. Does she like cum in her mouth?

TheUglyHusband: I think maybe. Do you like cum in your mouth?

SecretChloe: Yeah I love it. I want your cum in my mouth.

TheUglyHusband: You're gonna get it girl
But not today.

Chapter 64

It's been a big weekend. Claire and I are both tired and sapped, but when I take my clothes off to go to bed her eyes widen again.

I'm not in the mood - for the first time in weeks, it seems.

But as she leans over and kisses me, insistently.

I can't remember the last time she did that.

Well then.

I'm ruthless. As well as the slow, hard grind she likes, I pound her with my entire length, hard and fast and furious. Being lighter and fitter means that I can pump a lot harder, for a lot longer, without tiring out.

I push myself. I push her.

I wrestle her into different positions, then cycle through them all again.

Towards the end, she has her face in the pillow, biting and swallowing her cries.

I'm sweating rivers. She has given up trying to

grind against me - she lays prone on her belly, her fingers wrapped in the sheets, while I monkey-fuck her with everything I've got.

It isn't over quickly.

Afterwards, my body feels like it's made out of paper. I'm completely drained.

Claire tells me that she'll walk like a cowboy tomorrow.

Despite her feigned resignation, I can tell that she is pleased.

Chapter 65

Monday morning and it's kind of a relief to be heading to work. I feel like I've run a marathon.

When I get off the bus, I walk past a very tall, very attractive woman on her way to the gym.

Her long legs are topped with an almost non-existent pair of black shorts. I watch her hurry past, watch those long smooth legs working, watch that tight ass go about its serious business.

There is a warm spark in my chest, a shift in my ballbag. It makes me grin in delight; I'm exhausted, but I'm ready to go again.

I put my sunglasses on and walk to work.

Chapter 66

I'm ambivalent about public holidays. It's nice to have a day off work – particularly one that I'm getting paid for – but there's usually not much to do.

This Australia Day we've got a couple of choices; one of our old trash bag friends is having a barbeque at her house, while the mums crew is having an afternoon tea at one of the parks in the city.

Both options promise a chilled-out afternoon with the kids, the Hottest 100 playing in the background whilst the adults reach varying states of intoxication.

But the idea of being around our friends has exactly zero appeal.

Claire and I haven't done anything as a couple since New Year's Eve and neither of us wants to be in a situation that could easily turn awkward in front of our friends, or our daughters.

We're treading very carefully around each other

but it still feels like the situation could flare up on the slightest of pretences.

At the same time, we need to do *something*. Staying at home, cooped up together in our little house together all day, is a recipe for disaster. So I get online and check out the local events.

An hour later we all drive down to the Regatta at Lower Sandy Bay.

The day is bright and warm. There are a couple of thousand people wandering through the regatta, toting balloons, lining up for rides, trying to eat their soft serve before it melts. Kids run and scream and dash away from their frustrated mums while lazy dads recline on the grass cradling their Cascade Lights.

I buy the girls a plate of mini pancakes each and a glass of Sav Blanc for Claire, even though it's barely lunchtime.

I get myself a coffee and sneak off for a joint in the carpark.

SecretChloe: Any parties today?

TheUglyHusband: Yeah just arrived at one. Pretty tame. How about you?

SecretChloe: Yeah a big one down at a friend's family shack at Sandford on the beach

TheUglyHusband: Sounds cool. Have fun!

By the time I get back to the family, I've got a nice buzz on. The sunshine is cosy.

I love people-watching when I'm stoned, especially in summertime. And there is plenty to watch here too.

The girls lead us from ride to ride, stall to stall, until both Claire and I have an armload of soft toys and plastic fantastic. Little L wins a toy unicorn on the chocolate wheel, declares it her new cuddle toy, then promptly drops it in the dirt.

A couple of times I catch Claire watching me from the corner of her eye.

She doesn't say much, but as the afternoon passes she becomes more and more relaxed, even laughing at a couple of my lame jokes.

I buy her another wine. It's nice.

We line up for ten minutes to try a new pear cider. When we get it, Claire and I share the small white plastic cup it comes in.

The cider tickles my nose. I don't rate it, but Claire does, so I buy a six pack.

As I'm walking away from the stall, I pass a tall blonde woman dressed in active wear who flashes me a very friendly smile.

I smile back, but neither of us pause to say hi.

As I pass the cold ciders to Claire she frowns, looks away, doesn't thank me.

It's a struggle not to sigh.

If we're going to play happy families she could at least put some effort in.

I take the girls over to see the army helicopter.

Chapter 67

Later that night, Claire and I sit on the balcony sharing a joint. She's been quiet ever since we got home.

She tells me that she wants to talk about our relationship. I loosen my holsters and lean back, relaxed.

I know where she thinks this is heading; the same place our relationship talks always end up. She'll be crying and fuming, I'll be hiding quietly in some awkward spot - the rubbish-strewn gap between the shed and the fence is a favourite - wishing I was somewhere else, anywhere else.

But this time it doesn't go that way.

Straight off the bat, Claire asks me if I still want to be with her.

Even though it's a question I've pondered a lot myself recently, I don't have a quick answer.

She nods at my hesitation, as if she had expected it.

"I've really fucked it up this time, haven't I?"

There is no energy in her voice.

"Claire… there are two of us in this relationship."

She nods sadly.

"I don't know why you stayed with me all these years. You would be much better off without me."

"What are you talking about?"

A slow tear is rolling down her cheek, glittering in the dark.

"I'm broken. I can't go on like this anymore. It's just not working. Is it?" The last is more of a demand than a question.

"Actually I thought things were getting better." I cross my arms. "The last week or two, things were going ok… weren't they?"

"Yes." Husky and low, so low I barely heard it.

"So what happened?"

I hold my breath, sure that she is about to confess. If she tells me about Ronnie… will I confess as well?

"I saw you smiling at that woman today". She wipes the tear away. Her voice has changed. "She was pretty."

"People smile, Claire. You smile at everyone and for years you've told me over and over that it's not flirting…"

"But *you* don't smile at everyone. At anyone. Well, you didn't. I know you, Joe, I know what you're like. You usually would have scowled at her, probably scared her off. But today... you smiled back at her."

If anything, I'm surprised she noticed. It was a fleeting moment in a big crowd on a busy day.

But she's right. I smiled at a woman who had smiled at me.

I refuse to feel guilty.

"I have to be myself, Claire. I should be able to smile at somebody without feeling like I've done anything wrong... right? That's how it is for you, isn't it? It's just a smile."

"You *should*, you *should* be able to smile at whoever you want."

She's nodding, nodding, her bottom lip quivering.

"You always should have been. It's just another sign that I'm a fucked person, that I treated you so badly that you were scared to even *smile* at someone..."

I don't know what to say. I want to agree with her.

"For so long, our love has been the foundation of my world. It was so strong, so reliable, for *so* long... and I just started taking it for granted. I thought you would love me for ever and that was just the way it was. I didn't need to do anything, I didn't need to... I thought I could do what I wanted and you would still be there. After Christmas, I realised that you could take your love away… and the world disappeared from beneath my feet. I could see how angry you were. It made me realise just how *badly* I'd been treating you for the last few months. I don't blame you for not being able to stand me. But… when I thought about some of the things I've done - how awful… how *abusive* I was to you - I realised that it wasn't just the last few months. It was the *whole time* we've been together. I've *always* been unfair, always treated you so badly because I thought you would just… always be there. I thought I was a good person, but… I'm not. I'm really not. I'm fucked up, a fucked up person, a horrible, *abusive fucked up bitch. Why* did you stay with me?"

She looks up, her eyes shining in the dark.

"*How* could you love me?"

My mind is spinning. I kneel next to her chair and put my arms around her.

"I've loved you forever, Claire. A couple of months ago, I was broken too. I hit rock bottom. I realised how bad things were, and I couldn't believe that I'd let myself get to that stage. So I had to change, too. And I did. I'm a different person now, for better or for worse. I've changed, you must have noticed."

She nods and I take her hands.

"And now I'm fixing myself."

"Why would you stay with me then? If you're fixing your life. It's obvious you would be better off without me."

"I don't think so. I just couldn't go on the way I was any longer. I had to change. And I have."

"I don't know who I am anymore. I don't know who *we* are."

"So we work it out together. We help each other. We've been together forever, Claire. If we're going into a new stage of our lives, let's work it out together, let's help each other become the people we want to be."

Am I bullshitting her?

I don't even know.

She nods, sniffs, pulls me close.

Chapter 68

There's this guy on my bus almost every afternoon. He wears one of those fedoras that were briefly in fashion in Hobart seven or eight summers ago. He wears it proudly.

I put him at a few years older than me, but it's hard to tell. He dresses like somebody who used to be hip, for a little while at least.

He stares at the girls on the bus. Stares without subtlety, without shame or empathy.

I'm sure that I saw him lick his lips once.

Right now, I'm sitting behind a girl whose workout gear is sheer and tight. He's sitting across the aisle from us, eyeing her up and down, down and up.

She's very attractive... but she doesn't smell great. I noticed her fit figure as she was sitting down, but I didn't let my eyes linger.

Unlike him.

Her outfit is pretty revealing, sure, but she's just

a woman on her way home from the gym. She doesn't need this overweight, dated hipster leering at her bits, reeking of desperation.

He's literally staring at her, almost angrily.

I may be creepy, but I'm not that fucking creepy. Am I?

When the bus stops, we watch her stand up and straighten herself out. We watch her thread her way down the aisle and bounce off through the back door.

When the doors close, he meets my eye and gives me the barest nod, raising his eyebrows.

He doesn't quite wink, but he might as well have.

I'm too horrified to return his smirk. He rubs his chin with a lazy hand and looks out the window.

I get off at the next stop. I feel sick.

They say it takes one to know one... and he definitely looked like he knew one.

Another hyena.

Me.

Chapter 69

It's just after ten in the morning. I'm sitting at my desk, flicking through *X*.

SecretChloe has posted a pic. In this one, she's wearing a light pink slip and a pair of white denim shorts that look more like an afterthought than anything else.

The photo cuts off just above her lips, and you can see her cheeky smile, the black choker around her neck and the studded bracelet on her wrist.

I love knowing that it's really her. I can't wait to touch her again.

She's so fucking hot.

SecretChloe: First day back at school, no classes til next week though but still have to give the boys something to look at xxx

But I'm bored. I want to see more. So I give her some gentle encouragement.

TheUglyHusband: You're such a tease to those poor boys x

SecretChloe: shame that I only like older men lol

Then she sends me a private message.

SecretChloe: Got another threesome lined up for this arvo x

TheUglyHusband: Two big cocks for you girl?

SecretChloe: Yeah neither of them are small

TheUglyHusband: Awesome... tho I'd rather you were getting mine lol I hope they fucking pound that pussy x

SecretChloe: All I'm wearing is a little pair of shorts and a t-shirt. As soon as they pick me up I'm going to tear them off!!! They told me they are going to smash me.

TheUglyHusband: Hmm you're so bad I hope that naughty little mouth gets pumped

I'm so fucking turned on.

The morning drags out. The heat is getting to me. My office feels like its getting smaller with every humid breath.

SecretChloe: Just got home and OMG all my holes got pumped

TheUglyHusband: Unf your ass as well?

SecretChloe: Oh yeah they had my ass

The thought of it gets me rock hard. I can't stand it. I need air.

None of my workmates speak as I get up from my desk and head outside.

There is a big park near my work and even in the midst of this hot dry summer the grass is lush and cool. There are folks scattered all through the space but two in particular catch my eye; two ladies sunbathing, both in bikinis. Tourists, probably, from the massive cruise ship that's hulking over the docks. I lay down, not too far away.

The sun feels great. I resist the urge to tear off my work shirt.

TheUglyHusband: I'd love to sneak into your room one night. hold you down and use your pussy

SecretChloe: Fuck me with a pillow over my face

TheUglyHusband: I'm going insane. So goddamned horny.

SecretChloe: Is your cock hard?

TheUglyHusband: So fucking hard. I'm in the park and there are two girls sunbathing right near me. Torture!

SecretChloe: What park?

TheUglyHusband: The big park near Salamanca

SecretChloe: As soon as the sun comes out and it gets hot, I get even hornier. Take a pic of the girls for me.

Now there's an idea. A terrible idea.

I'm not sure if I can get arrested for taking a photo, but I don't really want to find out.

But it's so hot. I'm so randy. The girl in the black bikini has a delicious figure.

I'm down the hill from them. They're lying on their slim bellies with the sun on their backs. My phone's camera has a pretty decent zoom, it turns out. After several attempts, feeling as creepy as they come, I manage to get a half-decent photo.

I send it to SecretChloe.

TheUglyHusband: I want that ass!

SecretChloe: i want it too! I wonder if she has been laying like that before as a guy pushes his cock in her ass

TheUglyHusband: I hope so!

SecretChloe: Do you ever just look at people and wonder if they go crazy in bed lol

TheUglyHusband: Ha-ha yep all the time. Would you like to share her with me?

SecretChloe: I could pull her bathers aside and lick her pussy

TheUglyHusband: Mm fuck yeah then I would come around behind you and put my cock deep inside

SecretChloe: Deep inside my ass

I have to stop talking to her. I have to go back to my office.

I'm so fucking randy. I've been hard for hours

and it's only the early afternoon. I don't finish work for three hours. My balls ache. My jeans feel so tight.

I doubt Claire has any idea what she's in for tonight.

Chapter 70

I don't think I could ever find Claire physically unappealing, no matter how badly she treats me. She's a very attractive woman.

Watching her curves glide around her kitchen turns me on. Watching her slip her sauvignon-blanc with shining lips turns me on. Watching her exit the bathroom with nothing but a white towel wrapped around her turns me on.

I check in on the girls just after nine. Little K is snoring away, a sewing machine hum. Big M is as still as a statue. I close their bedroom door tightly.

Claire is sitting on the edge of our bed, blow-drying her hair, lit by her bedside lamp, the white towel loose around her body. I watch her for a moment, her damp hair falling about her tanned shoulders, her lovely legs crossed, then I back out of the room.

In the darkness of the hallway, I quickly strip off my clothes, leaving them in a pile near my feet.

The air-conditioned warmth feels good and so does the soft carpet beneath my feet. Anticipation makes my blood pound, and I'm already stiffening when I push open the bedroom door.

Claire doesn't look up, so I climb onto the bed and kneel behind her. When she sees my reflection in the mirror, she switches off the hairdryer with a smile.

Her damp hair tickles my lower belly as I gently pull her head back and lean over to kiss her. Her lips are soft and welcoming.

As our tongues circle each other, my hands pull the towel open and away. Her breasts are pale above her tanned belly and I reach down take the weight of one in my hand, grazing her nipple with my thumb.

Her tongue is more insistent as I raise my hand to her neck, then to her cheek. Breaking off the kiss, I gently pull her face down so that she can see her reflection, naked in the lamplight.

"Look," I whisper in her ear. "You're fucking *gorgeous*."

She leans back and my hard cock presses against the soft skin of her back. We kiss again, and this time I take both of her breasts in my hands. She sighs and opens her mouth wide for my tongue.

Reaching down, I drift my fingertips along her tanned thigh then scoop my fingers beneath her knee, raising her foot onto the bed so that I can see her lovely pussy in the mirror.

She looks incredible, her legs spread wide, her eyes closed, her tongue wet against mine. I squeeze her nipple with my free hand and she gasps a little.

"Look," I whisper again.

She does.

My fingertips have danced back up her thigh and they gently tickle over her labia, pressing her clit for the briefest moment before opening her lips, finding her dampness.

She shivers when I run my fingertip over her pink, tights walls, and her hands grip my bicep. Her half-wet hair has fallen over one eye, but she still watches herself in the mirror as I slide my fingers inside her.

"You're fucking *amazing*," I tell her, curling my fingers inside her pussy.

She whimpers, so I roll her nipple between my fingertips then reach back to take a handful of her hair. Pulling her head back, I kiss her forcefully, giving her the thickness of my tongue while my fingers fill her from below.

My cock is straining against her back. The feeling of her warm skin makes my brain numb.

Holding her hair, I move around beside her and direct her head down. She obediently pushes out her tongue and I slide my cock over it, from the base to the tip.

The rough wetness of her pink tongue fills my body with relief… and hunger. My fingers quiver in her tight cunt.

She opens wide for me and I push my cock into her waiting mouth. She sighs again as she wraps her lips around me and I ease into her warm throat, sighing happily. She sucks at my hard flesh, her tongue working rapidly, her lips tight around my shaft.

As she begins to move faster, I start thrusting slowly with my fingers, pressing my palm against her clit, curling my knuckles against the back wall of her pussy. She groans, and I pull the hair out of her eyes so she can watch us in the mirror.

My fingers are growing slick, sparkling in the lamplight, my wet cock disappearing into her mouth, reappearing, disappearing again.

She watches us with the same rapt attention that I do, and lifts her other foot onto the edge of the bed, spread wide, my hand working between her thighs.

"You look so fucking *good* with my cock in your mouth."

She hums in agreement and stares at the mirror as I push all the way into her throat.

My fingers are moving faster and her hips are

rising off the bed to meet them, her soft moans getting louder, her gorgeous breasts rising and falling with her quickening breath.

With one hand wrapped in her hair, the other wrapped in her pussy, I play my wife like a warm, soft instrument, driving my cock into her hungry mouth. Her pussy shivers against my palm, then her thighs are shaking and she's grabbing at my wrist.

"Cum for me," I command her. "Cum with my fucking cock in your mouth."

She does, closing her eyes and squealing around my shaft, her hips rising and falling, rising and falling. Her hands grip my implacable arm and she pushes against my fingers.

My cock falls out of her mouth, dripping with her saliva, and she pulls her hips back. I press my wet fingers against her clit and she shudders again.

"My... fucking... *god...*"

Her body is soft and boneless as I push her back onto the pillow, spinning her around beneath me. I put my hands on her thighs and spread them wide.

Her pussy glistens, welcoming, and I drag my wet shaft over it, the maddening softness taking my breath away.

"Fuck me," she gasps. *"Please* fuck me!"

I lower my cock into her wetness and groan as

my hard flesh pierces her.

Our bodies fit together perfectly.

I lunge into her, driving my shaft deep, sighing as my balls push against her warm ass. She clutches at my hips, pulling me deeper, and I grind my cock against her soft walls.

Her soft whimpering drives me wild and I thrust again, hard, harder. Soon she is crying out, her hands clutching at the bedsheets as her breasts bounce hypnotically, her whole body flexing against my plunging cock.

There is sweat prickling on my forehead and my back as I work her body. The sight of my wet cock driving into her gorgeous little cunt brings me to the edge, and I slow down, catching my breath.

She writhes beneath me, eyes wide, lips quivering, and I drag my iron dick in a slow rhythm against her back walls. After a few slow rocks, she is shaking again.

I keep my pace steady, watching her body rise and fall, glancing at the mirror as she cums again, this time around my shaft.

Once she stops shaking, she collapses back on the mattress, her breath coming in ragged gulps. There is sweat shining between her breasts and I lean down and taste it with my tongue. Her heaving nipples fascinate my lips and I reach up to squeeze her other breast with my hand, my cock swelling against the softness of her pussy.

"Your turn," she whispers, her voice rasping.

"My turn," I agree, withdrawing from her.

She gives a gentle gasp of surprise as I push her legs down and climb up the mattress to straddle her ribcage, but when I push my impossibly stiff shaft between her gorgeous tits she squeezes them together with her hands, engulfing my rude cock in her perfectly pert, smooth cleavage.

She watches me with a curious smile as I slowly rock back and forth, fucking the softness of her tits. It feels incredible around my bulging, sensitive shaft.

Turning her head to watch us in the mirror, her mouth drops open at the sight of my sweaty body fucking her tits. Her hips raise off the bed again, encouraging me, and her hands squeeze tighter.

Reaching down to grip her hair, I lean forward so that my cock rests against her face. She turns back to me and for a moment there is reluctance in her eyes. She's always baulked at her own taste, but I'm having none of it.

"*Open.*"

My grip on her hair tightens.

She opens her mouth, and when I dip my cock in, her eyes roll back in her head.

I can't help but groan loudly at the feeling of her tongue on my sensitive shaft. My body takes over, thrusting faster and faster between her lips as she whimpers and squirms.

My body is thrumming, buzzing, and I pull back and put my cock between her tits again. She gasps up at me, smiling as I drag my cock over her soft skin, then lean forward again into her mouth. This time she takes me willingly, sucking hard, her lips slurping around my shaft.

It feels like a ten=pound stone is rolling off my balls and I push into her throat, holding her down, as the first sprays of cum electrify the tip of my cock.

She moans around my spasming cock and gasps when I quickly pull out of her mouth.

Hot white cum blasts out my cock, splashing across her flushed cheeks, across her pillow and the bedhead.

I'm shaking and gasping and when she grips my cock in her hands and squeezes I can't help but cry out.

My thick juice falls onto her lips, on her neck, and she wriggles below me, caressing my balls and squeezing my shaft as more cum drips out of me and onto her perfect soft tits.

My body is filled with light and air. My head is a balloon full of helium. My cock strains and spasms, dripping more thick cum onto her chest.

Claire watches my cock with fascination as she

squeezes out the last few pearls, humming as they drip onto her. She glances at the mirror, lifting a finger to the cum on her face, touching her lips, her breasts.

As I catch my breath, she massages my juices into her breasts, her cheeks flushed, her hair still damp.

I manage a chuckle as I back down the bed, taking her by the wrist and pulling her to sit upright. My cum drips from her chin as I turn her face to the mirror.

She stares at herself in something like wonder.

"Now," I breathe. "Now you look fucking *amazing.*"

She turns to look back at me and I kiss her softly on the lips.

My lovely wife is lost for words.

I chuckle again and climb off the bed, walking out of the room, leaving her to her own messy reflection.

That night, I slept like a baby.

Chapter 71

The rest of the weekend was incredibly boring. Claire woke up with her period on Saturday morning. Despite her grumbles and her nausea, I caught her smiling at me more than once when she thought I wasn't looking.

I felt delightfully light and limber, so I took the girls to the park and enjoyed the sunshine on my face, then cooked us up a huge succulent meal of pork ribs and fried rice.

After a walk around the block and a steaming hot bath, I went to bed without even glancing at my phone.

Claire was already asleep.

Chapter 72

M onday morning.
    While I'm on the bus to work, I read a couple of weekend posts from SecretChloe that I had missed.

SecretChloe: Is four cocks too many for one girl? Gonna find out today!

SecretChloe: Perfect day for fucking!!

I get the feeling the posts are meant specifically for me, but I don't favourite or retweet them like I usually do.

I'm too deflated. Things are going back to normal.

My anger at Claire is fading into the easy numbness of suburban day to day. We haven't fought in weeks. The girls seem happier than they have in a long time.

A girl sits on the seat in front of me. I've noticed her a bunch of times of course - a few years younger than me, lank blonde hair, covert eyes, dressed like Kurt Cobain. In another time, I would have thought she was gorgeous.

I've tried to catch her eye a few times to no avail. She usually sits up the front, but not today - this is the closest I've ever been to her.

I notice a couple of things; her thin woollen cardigan is Camilla & Marc. Just under her collar, around the back of her neck, there is a lace hem. Whatever she's wearing under that cardigan has a fancy trim.

And her hair smells like my childhood.

Breathing her in, I'm struck by a sudden nostalgia that lingers long after she has scampered off the bus.

Not nostalgia; it's a longing for a time that never was, a yearning for a life that I can't quite imagine clearly yet feels more tangible than this one. This world seems insubstantial. Other worlds are within reach, hiding just behind this foggy veil of rainy morning mist and metro bus musk. Other times, other lives, all of them are beckoning, none of them are real.

I get off the bus and walk to work.

Chapter 73

Things are sliding backwards.

It's been days since I last spoke with SecretChloe. She hasn't made any posts either. I know that I need to reach out to her so that I don't fall off her radar completely... but my excitement is fizzling.

I want to fuck her again, of course... but it's not enough.

I didn't set out to have an affair. This isn't about cheating on Claire. It's not about going tit for tat.

Six weeks ago I was ready to throw my life away, or at least risk everything to change it.

I want to feel wanted, desired, coveted.

Now that Claire seems happy, I'm settling back into the same old same old, day in, day out.

I can't just go back to hoping things will get better eventually. That's the road to suicide. Maybe I won't arrive there tomorrow, but I will one day.

And that just will **not** fucking do.

Chapter 74

SecretChloe: A bit hard to concentrate in class when just before I walk in I get sent a pic of a guys huge rock hard cock!

It sounds like she's keeping busy.

I, however, am not. Faced with the prospect of another quiet Friday night at home, I'm getting desperate for a bit of excitement.

TheUglyHusband: Have you ever eaten pussy?

SecretChloe: Has your wife ever eaten pussy?

TheUglyHusband: No lol

SecretChloe: I've eaten one of my friends out and that's it.

TheUglyHusband: Did your friend have a nice pussy?

SecretChloe: She had a great pussy. We had a movie night at her house and we started fooling round on the couch late that night

TheUglyHusband: Sexy. Did she lick you too?

SecretChloe: No but fingered me. I made her

cum like 10 times. yummmmm

TheUglyHusband: Oh fuck my cock is aching.

SecretChloe: Her mum came out at one stage to see if we was ok. Luckily we heard her coming lol

TheUglyHusband: Lol sounds like she heard you coming too

SecretChloe: Haha. I was on my knees on the floor while she was on the couch with her feet on my shoulders when we heard her, so I jumped up and put the blanket over us

TheUglyHusband: Wow

SecretChloe: Then we waited 5 mins after she left before I got back to it lol

TheUglyHusband: I can't even.

SecretChloe: She was lifting her legs right up! I gave her ass hole a lick but she said it tickled too much

TheUglyHusband: Did you put your fingers in her?

SecretChloe: Of course I did, only two though

TheUglyHusband: Hmm tight and wet

SecretChloe: Oh yeah she hadn't had much action so she was so tight and that's why she came so many times too

TheUglyHusband: Delicious. I love working open a tight pussy with my tongue so much

SecretChloe: Hahaha I was fingering myself

when I was eating her and made myself cum too

TheUglyHusband: That's so fucking hot my brain is breaking lol. I would give anything to see that

SecretChloe: Two girls going at it? My face was covered in her juices

TheUglyHusband: I want to fuck you while I taste her sweet juices

SecretChloe: That can be arranged sexy. I can taste her right now

TheUglyHusband: Arrange it.

SecretChloe: lol. My pussy is soaking.

TheUglyHusband: I'm gonna hold you down and tongue fuck you until you can't stand it.

She sends a photo; her pussy is neatly shaved, delightfully pink between her fingers.

SecretChloe: oh fuck i need to cum.

She's not the only one.

But my boss is talking to me from across the room, and my screensaver is on... how long has that been on? I clear my throat before I answer his question. It feels like I'm blushing.

I put my phone on the desk face down and leave it there for the rest of the afternoon.

Chapter 75

SecretChloe: Getting some today. I even have dad dropping me off at his house lol. Told him that "she is a friend" lol

I try not to think about it as we drive over to the train park on Hill Street. Claire, the girls and I are heading to a birthday party for one of our friend's kids. Best behaviour required.

SecretChloe: Just on my way to his house now, dad said he will pick me up at 12:30 so I have a big few hours ahead of me

It's mostly the usual crowd, but there is a new face amongst them. She's wearing a simple summer dress that clings to her in the right places. She's laughing and relaxed and has a lovely smile.

As soon as Claire and I arrive, she gives me an appraising pout… probably similar to the one I'm giving her. Claire gives her a smile and a wave, but doesn't introduce us.

SecretChloe: Just having a rest and a big cold

drink now. Daddy has no idea his little princess has spent the morning bouncing and sucking on a big cock

I sit down at one of the barbeque tables and reply.

TheUglyHusband: Haha little minx. Lush way to start the weekend

SecretChloe: Dad just called me and said he is running late too, what a shame lol

TheUglyHusband: Hmm better get naked again x

SecretChloe: I never got dressed lol just sucking his cock while I'm waiting for dad to turn up

TheUglyHusband: Ah a nice slow suck sounds luscious

One of the yummy mummies, Kirsty tells me that I've lost weight. She gives my shoulder a squeeze and tells me that I look good, actually… before realizing what she is saying and trailing off awkwardly. She glances over at Claire nervously.

It's hard not to grin.

SecretChloe: What are you up to today, I'm in the car with daddy now

TheUglyHusband: I'm at a kid's party in some park lol

SecretChloe: That's no good, any hot mums there?

All of the mums are drinking champagne – the

kid is turning five, after all. The dad's hunch over their elbows and mutter to each other about surf spots and dance parties, whilst the kids scream their way from one end of the park to the other.

It's funny. Not one of these people have mentioned Ronnie to me. They're my friends, but some of them were out with Claire the night she kissed that motherfucker on the dancefloor. They would have seen it.

At one point I end up outside the park, smoking away from the kids, when I'm joined by two women from the party.

I've known Katie for years – she's one of Claire's best friends – but the other smoker is the woman I don't recognise. She lights up a long, skinny menthol cigarette and watches me chat with Katie.

"Oh!" Katie says eventually. "Joe, have you met Veronica?"

I extend a polite hand and she takes it. Her fingers are cool and thin, like her cigarette.

"You're Claire's husband?" she asks, looking at Katie for confirmation.

"I am," I give her an easy smile. "How do you know my wife?"

"Um," she says, her eyes looking this way and that.

I almost laugh out loud.

Katie saves her, rolling her eyes.

"Veronica's struggling," she confides to me with a grin. "She and her… friend… were having lines all night."

Veronica blushes but nods.

"MDMA?" I ask her.

She nods again, the cigarette burning towards her fingers.

"I bought a heap for a wedding I'm going to on the Peninsula this weekend. Had to test it out, you know."

Now I'm surprised, but only momentarily. Veronica looks very clean cut.

She also looks a little embarrassed so I smile and shrug.

"It sounds like a nice night in."

She nods demurely. "It was pretty chill."

I look into her eyes.

"Not all chill, I hope."

Her smile becomes a smirk.

"No. Not all chill."

Her cheeks are flushed with the lightest pink. She's looking at me appraisingly.

I nod approvingly, holding her gaze.

"Good."

She smiles, the slightest upcurl of a lovely pair of lips.

Then Katie shouts a greeting, making us jump. Some of the other smokers have found us and abruptly our threesome has become a group of chimneys.

I don't speak to Veronica again, but once we rejoin the party I can feel her puzzled eyes on me.

Claire doesn't speak to her at all.

Chapter 76

On the drive home, I ask Claire about Veronica.

"I've only met her once before," she shrugs. "You seemed to get along with her though."

There is colour in her cheeks.

I pretend not to notice.

"She seems pretty chill."

Not all chill though.

Thinking about Veronica and her friend getting high and getting naked has given me an idea.

A good idea.

Chapter 77

I roll a joint and take it into the back yard. Hobart is dozing in the late summer sunset.

I finally answer the question SecretChloe asked me hours ago.

TheUglyHusband: There WAS a hottie at the party. She had the naughty smile lol. A couple of the regular crew are pretty hot too but they're all my wife's friends.

SecretChloe: Have you fucked any of them?

TheUglyHusband: Not yet lol.

SecretChloe: Want to come and fuck me and my friend this weekend?

I almost drop my phone.

I read it again, all thoughts of Claire and Veronica and their friends forgotten.

SecretChloe: Friday night?

TheUglyHusband: Fuck yeah I wanna do that. Your place?

SecretChloe: Good. Yeah she's staying here

and my parents are going out for a few hours after seven.

TheUglyHusband: Nice. I'm hard now just thinking about it.

SecretChloe: She's so fucking hot, I can't wait to lick her juices off your cock

I'm gaping at my phone like an idiot. My head is light. My body thrums with adrenaline.

I could stand up and sing.

I could run through the air.

I could explode into million shards of light.

Instead, I put my phone in my pocket, finish my joint, and head inside for dinner.

Chapter 78

I'm hanging around.

I'm waiting, waiting all morning, all afternoon, all evening.

It's just a matter of getting Claire into the bedroom now.

Not long after the girls have gone to bed, she gives me the perfect opening.

"My back's aching… maybe you could give me a massage?"

"Sure."

"Really?"

"Let's do it now."

I lead her into the bedroom and push her onto the bed. She's surprised, delighted.

I take off her t-shirt and bra. While she nestles comfortably into the duvet, I strip down to my underwear.

Once she's settled, I climb onto the bed too, straddling her butt. Her skin is lovely, her back smooth and tanned.

I start slowly, pushing my thumbs into her shoulder muscles the way she likes. She closes her eyes and relaxes. I push my hands over her tanned back, soft and firm in turns, drawing patterns on her skin.

After a few minutes I reach for the nightstand and the little bottle of oil in my stash. I pour a bit into my palm, warming it up, then smooth my hands over her back again.

She wriggles on the bed with a deep sigh of pleasure, smiling into the pillow.

"I *am* being spoiled."

My hands glide across her skin, pushing and stroking, over her shoulders and down her back to the hem of her panties. She hums and pushes her ass up against my hard on.

"You like touching me, huh?"

Instead of answering I roll her onto her back and run my hands up her sides, over her ribs, around her breasts. I'm careful to leave a spot in the centre of her chest dry and oil-free.

My wife stretches her lovely body beneath my hands and eventually I shuffle down the bed and slowly remove her panties.

She twists a little with her usual self-consciousness but doesn't resist when I run my oiled hands up the insides of her warm thighs, massaging, stroking.

When I finally run a light finger over her lips, she sighs again.

I open her up a little with my fingertips, her flesh growing more and more pliable with every moment.

Then I turn away from her, reaching for the bedside table again.

Claire jolts, startled, and tries to sit up.

"What are you…?"

I shush her, ease her back down onto the mattress, then run my hand over her lower belly again.

With my other hand, I reach back into the stash and retrieve the carefully folded strip of tinfoil.

Her eyes widen as I shake a bit of cocaine off the foil to make a short line on the dry spot between her breasts.

"What's *that?*"

"Coke. Good coke."

"But where did you…"

"It doesn't matter."

She watches me, her mouth hanging slightly ajar, as I lean over and snort the line from between her tits.

Cold sunshine barrels into my bloodstream. My head rushes. My blood sings. My cock strains.

I kneel on the bed and pick up the foil again, working carefully to pour a line of coke along the top of my hard shaft.

Her eyes wide with disbelief, Claire lets me pull her forward. She licks her lips.

"Are you... is this..."

"Do it." I whisper, my voice rough.

She lowers her head and snorts the line of coke off my cock, licking it afterwards for good measure. She sits back, eyes bright, high colour in her cheeks.

I lay her back, then slide down the bed and blow warm air onto her pussy lips. She shivers as my tongue teases her lips apart and tickles at her hooded clit.

She tastes like fucking magic. I can't get enough.

I bury my face in her pussy, fuck her with my tongue, holding her hips while I lap at her wetness. She groans and pushes against me, moving her hips faster and faster until she pushes me away, gasping for breath, her hair sticking to her flushed face.

"Fuck me," she demands. "Put your *cock* in me."

"It's not ready yet."

I lay on my back, next to her on the bed. She sits up and watches, bemused, as I pick the foil up again and sprinkle another line of coke along my hard on.

She grins at me, shaking her head, then kneels on the bed between my knees. Pulling her hair over one shoulder, she snorts the line in one efficient sweep then eagerly takes my cock into her mouth.

My body melts. Every nerve is electrified. Even when her teeth scrape against me, it feels amazing. Her tongue presses urgently against my shaft and I wrap my hand up in her hair and thrust against her lips.

By the time she clambers up to sit astride my waist, my cock has turned to iron. I've never been so hard.

Her little pussy is soft, so impossibly soft and slippery and warm as it envelopes my iron, taking in every inch, wrapping it in maddening tightness that turns my brain to mush.

We fuck like animals.

I can feel every pulse of blood in my veins, every gasp against my cheek, every drop of her juices on my skin. My cock tingles and bulges and swells and plunges, my knob gliding against her tender flesh, my shaft pushing in her in all directions.

She leans back, giving me a full view of her sweaty, slender naked body, the muscles in her belly flexing and relaxing as she thrusts her beautiful pussy down onto my solid stone dick. The sight of her lips stretched around me is hypnotic and I press a thumb against her swollen clit, massaging it as she grunts and gasps.

I throw her off and before she can move I pounce onto her back, pushing her face into the pillow, shoving her legs apart so that I can thrust deeper into her warm cunt.

I hold her down and monkey-fuck her as fast as I can, ruthlessly pushing at her insides, stretching my cock into her as far as I can, further, shoving for every new depth, feeling her body mould and resist and relax and flex.

I pull her up onto her knees and kneel behind her, my cock sliding deep, my hands on her bouncing tits. I squeeze her entire body with my arms, squeeze her throat with my hands.

I shove my fingers in her mouth and she licks at them helplessly.

I throw her up and down on my shaft and her ass smacks against me, her pussy jerking my stiff cock in all directions.

When I cum it's like a plane landing. Our bodies jolt together, rough and unpredictable, then we slow down, smooth out, and she holds me tightly as our bodies come to a complete stop.

"Jesus fucking Christ, Joey." She says when her breath has come back. "What's gotten into you?"

"Sorry," I mumble, hazy headed and exhausted.

"Don't be sorry," she giggles. "I want you to do it again."

Chapter 79

I wake up hard, as usual.

But this time it's *painful*.

I stumble into the bathroom to see what's going on.

My stomach sinks.

There are half a dozen tiny sores on one side of my dick. Tiny cuts, grouped together in a small crescent.

I stare in dismay as my morning glory wilts. There's something weird about the crescent shape, some kind of orderliness about it that's confusing. Is there an STD that looks like that?

I've *never* had an STD.

I don't fucking want one *now*.

Possible explanations hit me in quick succession; did I catch something from Lisa or SecretChloe?

Will I get sick?

Have I passed it on to Claire?

Or has Claire passed it on to me?

Will these six or seven little marks be the final straw for our marriage?

I'm in the shower, staring at them, when I realise what the tiny cuts are, what that crescent shape means.

They're teeth marks.

Claire's teeth marks.

I think back to last night.

For the first couple of minutes after she licked the coke of my cock, Claire had gone wild. I vaguely remember her teeth scraping me in her eagerness.

Shit.

I earned these cuts.

They're superficial, but sensitive.

I put them away.

I hope to Christ that they don't take long to heal.

Chapter 80

The bite marks look even worse today.

If I get even slightly hard, they sting.

I'm uncomfortable on the bus.

I'm uncomfortable at my desk.

I'm uncomfortable.

I read a bunch of online articles that assure me that my knob isn't going to fall off. It's not very reassuring.

Take my advice: don't ever do a Google image search for penis injury.

Just *don't*.

Chapter 81

The marks aren't going away. If anything, they look even worse day by day as they dry off and darken.

There's no way they'll be gone before tomorrow night. No way I can hide them from SecretChloe and her friend.

They look like pox. I'm reminded of them every time I move.

Poxy.

And it's now been four days since I last came. My body has become used to regular release and now it feels like my balls could burst at any given moment.

It's turning me hyena.

Every second woman looks amazing. Their slender shoulders, resting high on the bus seats, seem to cry out for an embrace. A flash of supple thigh is enough to shut my brain down. I'm a glimpse of sideboob away from melting into a steaming, drooling mess.

    I need to work out harder.

    I need to heal faster.

    I need to be ready.

Chapter 82

I wake up with a feeling of dread.
I'm still sore.

My dick is still a mess.

I don't know what to do.

Should I put something on the cuts. a healing cream maybe? Would one of Claire's moisturisers help? Or would it do more damage?

Maybe I should ask her.

Maybe not.

I'm fooling myself. It's too late to do anything about it. Way too late.

It's not going to look any better by tonight.

I could cry.

I keep checking throughout the day anyway. Nothing changes, except that I'm slowly deflating, minute by minute, slowly fading away and becoming a shadow.

By three o'clock I've accepted that it's not going to happen.

I can't expect anyone to touch my dick in the state it's in. It looks diseased, even if it isn't.

Oh god I hope it heals.

TheUglyHusband: Hey sexy

SecretChloe: Excited?

It's so hard to type.

I've never wanted to write something less in all my life.

TheUglyHusband: I have to bail. My grandfather died. I'm driving to Launceston atm.

I'm only half-lying. My grandfather did die. About five years ago.

TheUglyHusband: I'm sorry. Totally gutted.

She doesn't respond.

I'm staring at my phone, my guts churning. Minutes tick by, then…

SecretChloe: Oh.

Then a few minutes later…

SecretChloe: I'm sorry about your pop. We'll have fun some other time.

TheUglyHusband: apologise to your friend for me too.

SecretChloe: lol im sure we'll still have fun x

I'm sure they will too.

I curse the lucky bastard who's getting a text message, an invitation, right about now.

I put my head on my desk and try not to scream.

Chapter 83

It's Valentine's Day.

The lover's day has never really meant much around here. In fact, we haven't marked the last couple at all.

For so many years I went to a tonne of effort – gifts, fancy dinners, getaways – with no reciprocation from Claire whatsoever, not even a fucking card or a massage or something, not even *once*...

Eventually I just gave up.

I figured she wasn't interested, or had cynically written the day off as a marketing scam. The first year that I didn't do anything, she didn't even notice that Valentine's Day had come and gone. I haven't planned anything for this year, either.

So I almost fall out of bed when she wakes me up with breakfast.

The girls bounce around on our doonah, excited by the novelty.

Eggs, toast, coffee and grapefruit juice.

I can't stand grapefruit juice, but I drink half of it anyway.

When I've finished eating, Claire pulls out three heart-shaped chocolates. One for me, one each for the girls. Nothing for her.

She watches us unwrap and gobble down the treats with the same small, satisfied smile playing on her lips the whole time.

In the afternoon we take the girls to the park at Cornelian Bay. They throw themselves from swing to slide and back again while we drink coffee and talk about the coming winter.

There is a sandpit. I let the girls bury me, even though the grit sneaks into my shoes and jeans. When I emerge from the ground moaning and grunting like a zombie the girls scatter, screaming laughter. Claire snaps a photo of Big M cleaning sand from my hair.

The other parents, huddled behind their phones, look at as us though we're mad.

Claire puts her arms around my shoulders and shakes the last cloud of grit off my shoulders.

"We're so lucky to have you."

She squeezes me.

It feels like she means it.

Chapter 84

It's been a few weeks since I checked in on Claire's *Facebook* page. I've been too caught up in my own stuff to even think of it.

And things have changed so much between us since Australia Day.

She's changed so much.

I guess we both have.

The cuts on my dick have healed, and Claire reaches for me almost every night now… but it doesn't feel right.

Why has she decided that I'm worth fucking again?

Is it out of habit?

A need for control?

Is she doing it because she wants to, or does she still think I'm going to break up our family and leave?

Am I really enough for her?

The thoughts niggle, distracting me from my

aching balls.

I need answers.

My laptop is still logged in to her *Facebook* account – once I log it out, I'll probably never get in again. I scroll through her inbox, glancing over messages from her friends, from her mum, from the groups she's in.

The most recent conversation is with Ronnie.

Ronnie: Hey gorgeous girl, I've been thinking about you x

Claire: Good, I've been thinking about us

Ronnie: Us?

Claire: You and me.

Ronnie: and hubby makes three.

Claire: omg lol

Ronnie: has he been getting you off

Claire: actually… he has. Does that bother you,?

Ronnie: ofc not, I'm glad ur getting some, gorgeous

Claire: well 've been fucking a lot but

Ronnie: but

Claire: sometimes I think about you when he's fucking me

Ronnie: omg lol that's so fucking hot youre sooooo naughty

Claire: I know, I'm bad

Ronnie: that turns me on so fukn much honestly.

Claire: well… maybe you should come over sometime and I could show you some of the things we do

Ronnie: anytime gorgeous, just say the word xx

I read it all again.

And again.

My blood runs cold.

Maybe there's nobody more scared of being robbed than a thief.

Chapter 85

I 'm back in the hole. I just want to be left alone. It's been ten days since our 'Class A' party for two.

Ten days since I last got laid.

I've barely even been hard. It was just too uncomfortable.

But today is a different story. Everything is *finally* back to normal down there.

I'm raring to go.

And that, of course, is the problem.

Despite things getting better, Claire still wants to fuck her new friend. She'd still prefer some stranger's dick over mine.

And I'll never get another chance for a threesome like the one I blew last Friday night.

Throughout all of this, the last thing I wanted to do was to add another missed opportunity to the list. But that's exactly what I've done.

I fucked it up by trying to show my cheating

wife a good time. I'll never forgive myself.

Summer is starting to lose its strength. The sun no longer stings my skin, the Hobart clouds are settling back into their sky. Soon Mount Wellington's shoulders will be spattered with snow.

It's all so fucking symbolic.

Chapter 86

I wish the women on the bus would stop smiling at me. What do they want from me?

This one has a snug denim jacket and a lovely neck, but that's not enough to work with.

I'm wavering.

I'm still working out most days, still losing weight, but apart from that I've already fallen back into the same old routine – work, home, bed, repeat.

Claire is gentle towards me, patient, pleasant.

I can see it in her eyes; she has weathered the storm and come out the other side.

And maybe that's what happened. She seems happier than she has in a very long time.

The glow of new beginnings, that sweet scent of potential, is fading with the summer.

All it took was two weeks without my cock for things to go back to the way they were.

Something's gotta give. I have to do something.

So I log on to *X*. Maybe one of the working girls I like will tour Hobart someday soon. I could make a booking and start saving. At least it will give me something to look forward to.

I check out my favourites first; carlydeeper, luluraringtogo, petitenympho and TiaMaria. None of them have mentioned any Tasmanian tours lately, or at all.

But the first post I read on TiaMaria's timeline makes me sit up a little straighter. It's a message that somebody has sent to her.

MissJazzJazz: Thanks for wrecking a 12 year marriage and the lives of four young children. You lowlife slut.

There's a reply from TiaMaria.

TiaMaria: Lowlife slut is already written on my gravestone baby, you'll have to do better than that xxx

MissJazzJazz: Please can we DM?

After that, a series of tweets from MissJazzJazz, all directed to TiaMaria, one after the other.

MissJazzJazz: i'm sorry, I just need to talk to you :(

MissJazzJazz: Please message me…

The tweets are coming in every twenty seconds or so. I can't look away.

MissJazzJazz: i'm sorry, i'm five months pregnant and just found out my husband has had an affair. feeling pretty suicidal right now

MissJazzJazz: Help me :(

MissJazzJazz: Pllease T I dont blame you at all. you were just doing your job, i just need answers about my husband - why he did this to me???

No response from TiaMaria. I wonder if she's seeing the messages come in. She must be seeing them.

But she doesn't reply.

I click on to MissJazzJazz's X profile. It's just a few minutes old. Her only posts are the ones directed at TiaMaria.

She has a profile pic though; it's a professional head shot, black and white, of a blonde woman in her early thirties. She's attractive in the photo, if not a little severe.

I can't help but notice that she looks a lot like Claire.

MissJazzJazz: nothing can wake me up from this nightmare. I'm done :(

MissJazzJazz: Please, i need to talk to you. I just want to understand some things, im rock bottom right now

The next post has a photo attached.

A bloody wrist.

It's a mess. Bright red grooves criss-cross her wrists, over her veins. The grooves have clearly been gouged out by fingernails.

Between the fresh wounds are dozens of thin white scars. The scars are all the same shape as the new scarlet ribbons.

This isn't the first time she's hurt herself like this.

But she's clearly asking for help.

MissJazzJazz: should I do it?

It's none of my business. I shouldn't get involved. I might make things worse. I might say the wrong thing and push her over the edge.

After all, I'm just another married man cruising for pussy online, like her husband.

Just another fucking hyena.

But… I also know the difference an anonymous ear on the internet can make. SecretChloe reached out to me - even if it was for completely different reasons – and it helped me.

Didn't it?

Shit.

I hit reply.

TheUglyHusband: No. You definitely shouldn't do it.

I watch my notifications.

She replies a minute later.

MissJazzJazz: so sad right now

Then I get a private message from her.

MissJazzJazz: Hi. thanks for caring

TheUglyHusband: Hi. It will be okay. Might

be hard to see it now, but you'll get through this

MissJazzJazz: I've spend most of my life building a facade - that im perfect, my familys perfect. and its all false. ive got no one to talk to, i dont want to be judged by others, just so close to saying goodbye. so much pain.

TheUglyHusband: I think I know where you're coming from. What anybody else thinks about you and your family is irrelevant. It's your life. People will want to help if they know you need help.

MissJazzJazz: im tired. everything is disappointing

TheUglyHusband: Everything is coloured by the way you feel right now. Put him aside for a moment, just think about yourself.

MissJazzJazz: Thanks. I just want TiaMaria to talk to me. i need some answers from the lies

TheUglyHusband: I'm sorry I don't know her at all. If I could get her to talk to you I would

MissJazzJazz: thats ok. you are sweet. thanks for trying to help

TheUglyHusband: Okay.

She doesn't reply so I click over to her profile. There is another photo – a box of Panadol on an outstretched hand.

MissJazzJazz: i hope this isn't painful for either of us, but its the only way out. best for our whole family

I almost laugh. Is she threatening suicide… with Panadol? I don't know if that's even possible.

Then I reread the post – I hope this isn't too painful for *either* of us.

Of course.

She's pregnant.

Panic starts to flutter in my chest.

She messages me again.

MissJazzJazz: i hope life brings you good things, you seem like a great guy

Keep her talking. Just keep her talking.

TheUglyHusband: Thanks…I almost ended it just a few months back. I'm rebuilding. It's possible to find new horizons even if it feels like you're deep in a hole.

MissJazzJazz: i have three kids and another one on the way. who the fuck will want to be with me now

TheUglyHusband: I have two. There will be plenty of guys, believe me… but you don't need anyone except your kids. Put them and yourself first and others will too. Have you talked to him? Does he know that you know?

MissJazzJazz: yes. He just lies. thats why i want to talk to her to know exactly how long he went

TheUglyHusband: If he didn't care about you, he wouldn't lie.

Now I'm lying to her as well, apparently.

MissJazzJazz: yes. he tried to tell me he just sat on a couch with her. but then i got deleted messages from his phone. which said a lot more. and multiple occasions. then he said he didnt see her outside. but then i found receipts on our credit card for apartments. i just want the truth thats all

TheUglyHusband: Yes you want answers and you deserve the truth. But you kind of already know what the truth is. Now it's about how to deal with it

MissJazzJazz: i dont know the truth. i need dates

TheUglyHusband: Will that info change anything though, or will it just make you feel worse? You know it's been happening

MissJazzJazz: i need the info

TheUglyHusband: Ok

MissJazzJazz: im scared now. ive taken lots of Panadol

I flick back to her profile. She has posted another photo. It makes my blood run cold.

The photo is one of her face – the same face that's in the profile pic, without the styling and professional lighting.

She is staring at the camera, dead eyed. Her face is pale, her hair a birdsnest. She looks exhausted.

A thin line of blood is runs from her nostril to her lip.

MissJazzJazz: Hey TiaMaria I didn't know Panadol would give you a nose bleed.

While I'm reading the post, wondering what the fuck I'm supposed to do, another photo comes up. The same face.

There is far more blood, coming from both nostrils now.

Somehow, she looks calmer.

TheUglyHusband: Call an ambulance. Now. Don't wait.

No response.

TheUglyHusband: Please. Give me your address and I'll call it

MissJazzJazz: no

TheUglyHusband: Please call one. Paracetamol won't kill you any time soon. Get it out before it makes you really sick

Should I talk about the baby? Her other kids?

MissJazzJazz: okay. Tia is somewhat talking to me at least. i just need to know :(i cant move on from this state without the truth

TheUglyHusband: Good that she's talking to you. Get the pills out of your system so you can keep talking to her

Another pause, longer this time.

MissJazzJazz: ok im throwing them up

TheUglyHusband: Good

There's no way of knowing whether she's telling

the truth.

About any of it.

MissJazzJazz: im leaving X now. she wont talk to me. thanks for your help, you are a good person x

I'm very, very far from being a good person.

TheUglyHusband: Talk to me anytime. Remember this will pass

MissJazzJazz: thanks, whats your name besides TheUglyHusband. Haha

TheUglyHusband: I'm Joe. I'm learning that it's a weird world out there. It's hard to cut a path through it but not impossible

MissJazzJazz: nice to meet you Joe

TheUglyHusband: You too, wish it was under better circumstances. Put yourself first.

MissJazzJazz: Thanks, I'm going to have a shower now. Feeling a bit more sane. Xxx

And then she's gone.

I'm kind of relieved. I hope she's going to be okay.

I check in on her account ten minutes later; all her posts have been deleted. Our conversation disappears a minute later, followed by her entire account.

She's gone. It's as if she never existed at all.

I wonder about the scars on her wrists.

I wonder if she fakes suicide attempts whenever

she's upset.

I wonder if she's still alive tonight.

I'm not sure if I can do this anymore.

Chapter 87

I wake up thinking about bloody wrists.

Claire kisses me on the cheek before I get out of bed. I can't remember the last time she did that.

Once I'm on the bus, I start deleting.

I delete my fake *Facebook* account and my *Locanto* account.

Then I go through my *X* account and unfollow almost everyone.

All the call girls, all the cam girls, all the lonely housewives and horny women I've been keeping tabs on the past couple of months.

I delete them all.

All except for one.

Chapter 88

C laire is watching me work out.

"You know," she says, "I've never seen you look like this, in all the years we've been together."

I finish the set and relax back on my hands, out of breath.

"Look like what?"

She chuckles. "I can see your ribs. And you've got abs. None of your clothes fit you anymore."

I look down. It's true, I guess.

"That's a good thing, right?"

"It's a very good thing. You look great... but what brought it all on?"

"What do you mean?"

"I mean getting fit. Changing your diet, working out... it's great that you're getting healthier. I'm just wondering why you decided to do it."

I've kind of been waiting for this question.

"Well... I was having a pretty hard time at the end of last year, you know that."

Hard enough to want to kill myself.

Claire nods carefully. It's obvious she doesn't want to revisit that time.

"I was sick for a few days and then…. depressed, I guess. I wasn't eating properly anyway and by the end of December I'd lost a lot of weight so… I just rolled with it."

She nods, satisfied.

It's the truth, mostly; I can't tell her what my real motivation was. I didn't care about getting healthy. I certainly didn't care about living longer. It's nice to be setting a good example for the girls, but that didn't have much to do with it either.

She climbs down off the couch onto the floor next to me, moving like a leopard.

"You look amazing,' she croons.

"That's one of the benefits, I guess."

"There are quite a few benefits," she smiles, pushing me on to my back and straddling my waist. Her fingers trail down my belly's new curves.

"I gotta say… I'm reaping those benefits."

She wriggles her hips, pushing her pussy against me.

"Reap away," I tell her.

She pushes me back into the corner of the couch and runs her hands down my chest, over my belly. On to my belt buckle, which she wrestles and then discards like a disobedient snake. When my pants go, my hardness springs out eagerly and she teases me with her lips.

When she takes me into her mouth, my whole body wilts in relief.

I wrap my hand in her hair and draw my shaft along her lips, dipping the head into her cheek, playing it over her lips and chin.

Rock hard now, I fuck her mouth. My grip on her hair never loosens.

"*More,*" she gasps. "Give it to me!"

I want to give it to her.

I really, really do.

But it's not happening.

As sexy as it is, as much as I want to unload into her mouth... it's just not happening.

She works away with her tongue and her hands, watching me, waiting.

I can see her wondering why I'm not getting there.

Same thing I'm wondering.

She doesn't give up easily.

Her fingers tickle my balls and squeeze my shaft as her tongue flicks my head... but nothing gets me close.

I run over my stock of fantasies. I imagine I'm being licked by SecretChloe, by Lisa, by the girl from the bus. A cast of dozens flicks through my mind.

None of them can help.

She keeps going… but I'm not coming. I can't cum. I just can't.

I fuck away at her mouth like my soul depends on it… but I'm damned.

Damned and doomed.

Chapter 89

It's cold and wet. Aside from a remnant mugginess, Summer has given up the ghost.

People on my bus are wearing thick jackets, beanies, heavy shoes. They'll dress this way for the next nine months. I like Hobart, but I don't like the way the seasons roll out. Summer is always so short.

This summer, of all summers, felt like the shortest.

I flick through SecretChloe's timeline, morose.

She's written me off. I'm sure of it. And why wouldn't she.

I pause on the photo of her perfect pussy. It's a delicious tease of sensuality and sexuality – her skin looks softer than a Botticelli cherub, yet I know of some of the things that skin has done. I remember its maddening tightness. I want to run my hands over that skin.

I message her. I can't help myself. I don't expect

a response though.

TheUglyHusband: That pic of your gorgeous pussy is driving me insane.

It hangs there in cyberspace.

To me it reads of loneliness, attrition.

Desperation.

But to my surprise – and delight – I get a reply.

SecretChloe: You want to taste my juices?

As if nothing ever happened.

A light flicks on in my chest, a flutter of excitement.

TheUglyHusband: You know I do. I could eat your peach for days.

SecretChloe: I want your big cock in my ass again.

TheUglyHusband: I can come over and give it to you tonight…

It won't be easy to get away tonight, but if she's up for it I'll think of something. I'm already hard at my desk, thinking of it. I need longer with her this time.

I need to show her that I'm worth waiting for. I need to prove to her that I'll turn up.

But she doesn't message back straight away and when she finally does, it's not the answer I want.

SecretChloe: Not tonight. Soon.

Disappointment and relief mix together.

'Soon' is probably the best I could have hoped

for.

It's more than I deserve.

I need to play it cool.

TheUglyHusband: Very soon I hope. I have so much cum for you right now.

SecretChloe: Save it up baby, I want every last drop.

And she's gone.

Chapter 90

C laire and I have been fucking for over an hour but I just can't cum.

In the end, covered in sweat and flopping listlessly around the bed, Claire just gives up. She has had three or four orgasms and I can see that her energy is spent.

I turn her this way and that, trying to get deeper, harder, softer, to no avail.

She melts on to the bed, crossing her damp thighs, looking up at me with eyes I can't read.

I'm trying to catch my breath, standing next to the bed, waving in the air.

"Had enough?"

She hesitates.

"Maybe we could have a break."

"Okay. I wouldn't mind a smoke actually. I'm not finished with you though."

She forces a smile.

"I might be asleep by the time you come back.

I'm pretty floppy now." She can tell I'm not impressed. "But don't let that stop you."

It's not the first time that she's suggested having my way with her while she sleeps but... I tried it once, years ago, and it just felt... wrong. Consent is not even in the same league as enthusiasm.

I'm still hard ten minutes later as I'm smoking a joint on our balcony. She doesn't get out of bed.

On a whim, I take a few photos of my junk – hard, proud, glistening with Claire's juices. They turn out ok, especially in the indirect light.

Mindlessly horny, I open up *X* and send one to SecretChloe.

TheUglyHusband: So ready to fuck your little pussy

She doesn't usually reply this late, but she does this time.

SecretChloe: Oh fuck I want that cock inside me right now.

That cock is standing up in the night time breeze, ready for her.

My phone glows as I type.

TheUglyHusband: I would fucking pound you with it. So ready to explode.

SecretChloe: I hope you're saving it up for me?

TheUglyHusband: Yeah baby girl. You better get it soon though.

There's no response and after a little while I

deflate. I don't flick over to PornHub, even though the pressure in my balls is starting to make me feel ill.

If she wants it all, she'll get it all.

Every last drop.

Chapter 91

I'm sitting at my desk, just before lunchtime, when I get a message from SecretChloe.

SecretChloe: Hey sexy

TheUglyHusband: What's up babygirl?

SecretChloe: lining up some more playtime this weekend.

Another threesome? I really don't want to know about it. Is she punishing me?

TheUglyHusband: sounds awesome

SecretChloe: Good. Can you come over tomorrow night?

Wait…

What?

I'd given up on getting a second chance at SecretChloe and her secret friend… yet here it is.

SecretChloe: You wanna come and share my body? So horny already!

For an odd moment I'm jealous of her.

If she wants a threesome, all she needs to do is send a couple of text messages.

Why can't it be that easy for me?

Then I realise; it *is* that easy for me, apparently.

Nobody would ever want to fuck you.

But that's not true anymore.

There *are* other women out there who would put up with me.

There *are* other women out there who might be interested in me.

There *are* other women who might want to fuck me.

All I have to do is say *yes*.

TheUglyHusband: Holy fucking shit YES that sounds so goddamned hot.

SecretChloe: lolol gooood! I want your gorgeous cock in my ass. Does that sound okay to you?

Sound okay?

I'm rock hard.

TheUglyHusband: you know it does. I'll need your little mouth too

SecretChloe: you wanna cum in my mouth baby?

She sends an address next, a flat in Bellerive.

SecretChloe: Get there just before nine. After that we'll be too busy to answer the door

TheUglyHusband: I'll be there x

I'll be there all right.
Nothing could stop me.

Chapter 92

I wake up with a hard on that feels three feet long. Excitement balances on the base of my spine, radiates out from my lower belly.

Claire is humming happily as she cooks breakfast, gliding through the house like a starling on a warm summer breeze. I can't look at her.

I get the girls dressed in a matter of minutes and then I'm gone. When the front door closes behind me, I let out a huge sigh of relief.

The world is out here waiting. I'm giddy with excitement.

There's a really strong compulsion to tell everyone I see about my plans for tonight, about the two young women who will be waiting to get wild with me.

Nobody else would have you.

Bullshit.

I'm *so* fucking ready for this.

I bounce on my toes the whole time I'm at the

bus stop, the whole time I'm at work, the whole way home again.

It's all I can do not to laugh and clap.

It's the last weekend of summer.

So much has changed – no.

I've changed so much.

Nobody else would ever want to be with you.

I've proven that particular opinion wrong and I'm ready to begin the next stage of my life.

Bring it *on!*

Chapter 93

T he traffic over the bridge seems different
tonight.

Red lights blur past, busy drivers on their way
to somewhere else. They feel like distant kin,
fellow soldiers in the battle against implacable
Time, partners in the fight against the void. It feels
like we are connected, like we all have something
in common. Maybe our anonymity.

The world feels noir. I'm as cool as they come,
with one hand on the wheel. The stereo is pulsing
out *Grimes*, deep and moody by the dashboard
light.

This is it.

The address SecretChloe gave me is a small red
brick flat, the last in a line of three.

I drive past, turn the next corner and park.

Deep breath.

Check myself in the rear-view mirror.

It's too late to do anything about my worn old

face, years too late. I smirk at my reflection, summoning bravado.

There it is. *Hey* – I think I know that guy.

Deep breath, then I'm out of the car, shutting the door, walking away, just an average guy on his way to a threesome with two gorgeous young women.

No biggie.

I weave my way through the cars parked outside the flats and march up to the door. Another deep breath.

But before I can knock, the door is pulled open. My wide grin falters.

A stocky bloke, older than me, shorter than me and quite a bit balder than me, looks me up and down. He must be in his late fifties or early sixties and bears a passing resemblance to Tony Abbot, the conservative ex-Prime Minister.

His sneer is aggressive.

"Who the fuck are you?"

"Sorry." I tell him. "I've got the wrong…"

"Clarry!" comes a girl's voice from inside.

SecretChloe's voice.

"Don't be an asshole! Let him *in.*"

Clarry sneers at me again, sullenly this time. He takes a step back and nods me in. He's wearing a dark blue polo shirt and shapeless black slacks, like a Blockbusters uniform. Dark sweat stains cling to his armpits.

I hesitate. Who the fuck is this guy?

"Not gonna stand here all fuckin' night." Clarry scowls.

"Hang on."

I step past the angry little bald man and the door closes behind me.

Chapter 94

The apartment stinks of weed and mould and... something else.

Three steps take me through the threshold and into the light.

My stomach sinks.

SecretChloe is standing on a double bed in the middle of the room.

Not standing - *dancing.* She smiles at me as I come in, her hands clasped above her head, her hips gyrating a slow circle.

She's wearing next to nothing; a worn black bra with matching undies, thigh-high sheer stockings with a long ladder up one side.

Despite the trashy underwear and the heavy-handed make-up, she looks gorgeous. She could wear a potato sack and look gorgeous.

But I barely notice.

There are five men sitting around the room, watching her.

None of them pay any attention to me, frozen in the doorway. Clarry roughly nudges past and sits down on the edge of the couch, making it six men.

Plus me.

A *pack.*

The bloke Clarry sits next to is of a similar age, at least sixty.

Sharing the couch with them is a huge guy in his mid-twenties wearing a stained white t-shirt that doesn't quite stretch all the way over his rolling gut. His lightly coloured, fuzzy beard has spread over his double-chin, making him look like he doesn't have a neck. Something tells me that it's his apartment.

The next guy is sitting cross-legged on the floor. His black leather vest is covered in badges and his arms are just as covered in fading blue tattoos. There is a thick silver ring on each of his fingers and a matching one in his ear.

The last two guys are young, probably SecretChloe's age. The blonde one is so stoned he can barely lift his head, while the other is fiddling with something in a backpack.

"Is that everyone?" Clarry asks.

SecretChloe nods and smiles at me again.

"Good," somebody mutters.

I don't move any further into the room.

"Turn the music up." She commands.

The young guy with the backpack twists in his seat to fiddle with an iPhone. I recognise the song.

As a frantic faux-seventies sounds pulse through the small flat, SecretChloe moves with the beat. Her wrists twist this way and that and her body follows suit, her body writhing against the black cotton of her bra and panties.

The hyenas ease back in their seats, watching.

She turns her back to them and stretches forward, presenting them with her taut, firm flesh.

The old bloke next to Clarry starts squeezing away at his groin. By the time she has straightened up again, he has managed to pull down his zipper.

The men on either side of him don't bat an eyelid as he pulls out his cock and begins to stroke it.

It's time to leave.

It's clearly time to leave.

But my feet stay planted on the floor.

Chapter 95

T he music is fast and frenetic.
    SecretChloe moves through the room like smoke, swaying this way and that, trying to enchant us.

The hyena's eyes follow her every step.

She runs her hands down her body, over her black bra, down her lithe frame to her gyrating hips.

The kid with the backpack turns to watch her more closely and she raises her eyebrows at him. He gives her a short nod and she smiles, throwing her hands above her head.

The kid pulls something out his backpack, something made of dark metal.

A camera.

While he fiddles with the dials, the biker gets to his feet and stretches lazily.

SecretChloe turns to the biker and wriggles towards him, but before he can reach for her she turns away again.

"Wait."

The kid points the camera at her, gives her another nod.

"Okay."

She looks down the barrel as she dances, her arms waving slowly through the air, her smile bright, her eyes alive.

Turning her back to the camera, she squeezes a clasp and her bra falls away. She covers her pert breasts with her hands and turns to face the camera again, stepping down from the bed, flicking her eyes towards the biker.

The biker glares at the kid with the camera.

"Don't put *my* fuckin face in it or I'll cut yer fuckin *eyes* out."

"No faces." The kid doesn't flinch.

"Except *mine...*" SecretChloe croons.

She lowers herself to the floor, kneels in front of the camera, eyes fixed on the barrel.

Her lovely breasts shine in the dim light. She traces a finger across her lips, touches her nipple lightly, eases a hand down into her black panties.

The biker stands next to her, hands on hips.

Without turning away from the camera, SecretChloe reaches up and unzips him, biting her bottom lip

She eases his cock out of his black jeans and

there is a collective sigh around the room as she runs her tongue along it.

The biker's head rolls back on his shoulders. His dick is long and skinny, uncut, and she takes it into her mouth eagerly, squeezing it with her lips, rolling her tongue around his foreskin, eyebrows raised at the camera.

Abruptly the old guy next to Clarry is getting up as well, coming to stand on SecretChloe's other side.

Without missing a beat, she reaches up and takes his huge, wrinkled piece into her other hand, squeezing and caressing.

Meanwhile the biker has wrapped his tattooed hands in her dark hair. He tightens his grip as he pushes his cock deeper into her throat.

He holds her there while her hand works away at the old boy's hard rod, groaning. When he pulls back out of her mouth, a rope of salvia stretches from her lips to his wet knob.

SecretChloe grins up at him, keeps her hand on his shaft as she turns her attention to the other cock. The old bloke lets out a deep sigh as she kisses it. Her sweet, pink lips tease over his strong, stiff flesh. She has to open her mouth wide to get him in, but she manages it, her eyes twinkling.

She bears down on him, again and again, deeper and deeper, her breasts swaying prettily. The biker reaches down to cup a breast in his rough hand, while the old bloke strips off his shirt.

She turns back to biker and takes him into her mouth again; then back to the old guy, back and forth from cock to cock, her mouth and hands busy.

The camera whirs.

I can't look away.

My head is spinning and my stomach is roiling and my cock is getting harder and harder watching these two strangers share SecretChloe's mouth.

Her slender body is angelic.

Around the room, the other men are watching with rapt expressions. Clarry is leaning forward, eyes wide. Next to him on the couch, the fat guy's pallid cheeks are flushed and scarlet.

Only the young, stoned guy looks even slightly uncomfortable; our eyes meet for a moment and he immediately looks away into the distance. His cheeks are flushed as well.

The biker has stripped off his vest and t-shirt to reveal a skinny, tattooed frame. While SecretChloe licks the old boy's shaft, the biker reaches down into her panties, his rough hand rubbing her pussy.

She gasps and redoubles her efforts on the big, wrinkled cock in her mouth.

The biker's hand moves faster and faster.

Lifting her head, SecretChloe moans gently and the biker grabs her by the hair again, turns her face so that he can kiss her long and deep. Her hand finds his cock again as the old boy steps away to strip off completely.

The biker stands up straight and pulls SecretChloe to her feet as well. They kiss again, his skinny cock pushing against the flawless skin of her belly. He grips her head as his tongue plunders her mouth hungrily, without grace.

After a moment he pushes her back down. While she is bent over at the waist the old boy, fully naked now, kneels and gently tugs her panties down. She doesn't lift her head.

The old bloke gently runs his hands over her firm young ass, massaging, squeezing and softly spreading to reveal her neat little pussy.

When he leans in to push his tongue against those firm, delicious lips, her knees begin to tremble. She moves her feet further apart to let him get deeper and opens her mouth wide to take in the biker's cock as far as she can.

The old bloke leans back, his fingers massaging her wet lips. He nods to the camera boy, who quickly shuffles around to focus on SecretChloe's perfectly shaved pussy.

"Fucking *amazing.*" The kid whispers as the old bloke moves aside. I don't think he's even aware that he has spoken.

SecretChloe's hand sneaks out between her thighs to press against her clit momentarily and then she gently spreads her lips with two fingers. The biker is thrusting away at her mouth and her sex waves in the air as he rocks against her.

The old boy, standing now, puts his wiry hands around her pale waist. His old cock swings like a heavy pendulum and when he slides it over her pussy it comes away slippery and slick.

SecretChloe looks back at him, checks that the camera boy is there, then eases herself onto the old boy's thick shaft.

They both groan as he squeezes into her tight flesh.

There is a shaky sigh from across the room.

The stoned kid looks like he might cry.

Clarry leans back on the couch, his hand squeezing his crotch. The fat guy already has his cock out and his heavy breathing rattles.

The biker puts his hands by his side and watches his cock slide in and out of SecretChloe's mouth as the old boy fucks her from behind.

Her eyes are closed, her lusty cries muffled around the biker's stiffness. The old boy's face is as red as a beet, but his grip is strong on her soft white hips.

The three of them move in gasping tandem.

The old boy reaches down and takes her arms, pulling them back, using her wrists as reigns while he bucks against her. The biker puts one hand beneath her chin and the other on the back of her head, guiding her onto his cock as she bounces off the old boy's thrusting hips.

This is not the threesome I had in mind, but my cock strains against my zipper.

Chapter 96

I can't look away.

I wish to Christ that I was stoned or drunk or high.

I wish she had made it clearer exactly *who* was going to be shared tonight.

The old bloke pulls out, panting, his face red.

SecretChloe stands up straight as the biker gets down on the floor, laying back and propping himself up on his elbows. She stands astride him, a hunting goddess claiming her prey, then lowers herself down.

As soon as he's inside her, the biker starts thrusting away roughly. The old bloke, still breathing hard, pushes his rigid snake into SecretChloe's face. She takes him back into her mouth eagerly, her face flushed with lust.

Abruptly the couch groans and creaks as the fat guy stands up. He moves like a mountain, his dick poking out below the curtain of his filthy t-shirt

He waddles over to SecretChloe and stands opposite the old bloke, ready for his turn.

SecretChloe looks tiny next to his bulging frame, but she doesn't hesitate to take him into her mouth.

The fat guy wheezes out an airy moan as his piece disappears between her lips. His hands tangle in her hair, but I doubt he can see her face over his hanging gut.

She works away as the biker pushes her down onto his skinny length. The old bloke leans over and takes her hand, guiding it back to his waving wand.

Abruptly she lifts her head away, gasping.

The biker's heels are thrumming on the floor.

"Fucking… *fuck*. Fuck!"

He gnashes his teeth like a rat. Tendons are standing out on his neck.

SecretChloe cries out once, twice, then flops into a boneless hunch.

The old bloke lifts her head and pushes his dick against her face. Eyes closed, whining, she opens her mouth and searches for her cock like a newborn looking for a nipple.

The biker is still groaning as his length flops out of her, his skinny piece even skinnier now and covered in both their mess. He nudges and she lifts herself up so that he can slide out from beneath her.

She is so busy with the old bloke now that she doesn't seem to notice the biker stand up and walk away.

"Turn around." Fat guy's voice is the thinnest thing about him. He puts a meaty hand on her shoulder. "Gimme your ass."

She slowly kneels on all fours, but as she does she looks over her shoulder.

She nods in my direction.

"He gets it first."

Six heads swivel to look at me.

"I promised him."

Fat guy gives me a filthy scowl. His ruddy face is even more flushed now and his beady eyes try to pierce me – but he backs off just the same. He wobbles around next to old bloke who grimaces with annoyance but doesn't move.

SecretChloe gets back to work, her head bobbing from one cock to the other.

Camera kid shuffles around to film her waving ass.

SecretChloe's pulls at her firm cheeks, opening herself up. The biker's cum is still coating her pussy as she slips a finger into her other hole.

Fat guy and old bloke watch her finger going in and out and then, in turn, look at me.

Camera kid and Clarry are looking at me too.

I haven't moved since I first walked into the flat. My jeans are still on, my belt still buckled. And my hard on is gone.

Chapter 97

I check with my hand to make sure, but it's *definitely* gone.

My balls are throbbing though, my body awash with adrenaline. There is sweat trickling down my spine.

The sight of SecretChloe - naked and on all fours, driving her finger into her ass, waiting for my cock - is fucking incredible.

But I've got nothing.

The camera whirs.

And now *she's* looking back at me too, her sexy pout turning into a frown.

Fat bastard puts his hands on his white whale hips.

"Fuckin come on then!" He gestures towards SecretChloe's ass.

She looks into my eyes from across the room.

"Come on, *stud*." She calls softly.

I hold her gaze.

For a moment, we might as well be the only people in the room.

In the universe.

And then – without a conscious thought, without reason or feeling – my body betrays me.

Looking into SecretChloe's lustful eyes, I slowly, apologetically, shake my head.

Her eyes are wide with surprise, but only for the barest second.

Emotions quickly play across her face, one after the other; confusion, embarrassment, anger… and finally, disdain.

She dismisses me, turning away, turning back to the two cocks that are waiting for her attention.

Abruptly all of the adrenaline flows out of my body and I'm weak, listless, like my knees might give way. I lean back against the wall, propping myself up.

Fat Bastard sneers as he eases himself around behind SecretChloe.

"Weak cunt."

He turns his back on me too.

But his words break the spell. Suddenly I can move again.

I move towards the door.

"What the *fuck?*"

The biker's voice cuts through the air like a blade. He's staring at me, fury and disbelief playing across his features.

"Where *you* going? You don't fuckin leave *now*."

I scan the room.

Clarry sneers nastily. The old bloke ignores me. Stoner kid has his face buried in his hands.

"Look man," I tell him. "It's not…"

"No. *You* don't fuckin talk. *You* do what the lady fuckin tells ya."

I'm shaking my head, inching towards the door.

I need to get out of here. *Now.*

"Fuck him, if he wants to go…" Clarry begins but the Biker cuts him off.

"He seen *all* of our fuckin faces! And *now* he wants to fuck off and tell the *cops*."

He takes a menacing step towards me.

"Don't worry," camera kid mutters. "I've got him."

The camera is pointed at me, the big oily lens showing my reflection.

The red light is flashing.

He's still recording.

Shit.

I should stop him, but my hand has finally reached the door handle.

"Why the *fuck* would I call…"

Biker lunges.

Shocked, I stumble backwards and my feet tangle together.

The tattooed man lurches at me, arms out-stretched, and I try to stop myself falling by holding the door handle but instead the door swings open…

… and cracks into Biker's head with a meaty, heavy thud.

He crumples to the floor, face down.

The room freezes.

The biker shudders once as I stand up straight. He doesn't move again.

A pool of blood spreads below his face, leaching into the filthy carpet.

He still doesn't move.

Old bloke is gaping at me. Fat guy is looking over his shoulder, trying to see, trying to not pull out.

I can't see SecretChloe's face.

But I can see the camera.

The kid is kneeling on the floor, not three metres away, his mouth hanging open.

The camera's red light is still flashing.

He's still recording.

My head is buzzing.

The biker isn't moving.

Suddenly the adrenaline is back, filling my body with electricity.

In three quick steps I swipe at the camera, catching it in my palm and wrenching it away from the kid.

He tries to hold onto it but overbalances instead, landing on the floor at the biker's feet.

The camera's in my hand. It's red light blinks.

I turn and bolt.

There is shouting and movement behind me, but I'm out of the flat and running down the street.

I don't look back.

I run.

I run like I've never run before. I couldn't have run like this ten weeks ago. I run until I reach my car.

I throw myself into the driver's seat and seconds later my tires squeal. I don't look in the rearview mirror.

I take a couple of back streets, then pull up in a McDonald's car park for fifteen minutes, anxiously watching the main road, looking at driver's faces.

I don't see any of the men.

They haven't followed me.

I'm okay.

I'm okay.

Chapter 98

I trudge across our front lawn.

A neat suburban lawn, scattered with toys. Work, bills, responsibility, respectability.

This is it. This is what I have to look forward to. Forever.

A lifetime of wondering who I might have been.

I push open the front door, kick my shoes off in the hall – and freeze.

Drunken laughter drifts from our loungeroom, curling around the cold stone that sits heavily in the pit of my stomach.

Claire is here, and she's not alone.

I steel myself and walk into the lounge… and my mouth drops open.

Claire is giggling on the lounge, her legs resting on Veronica's knees.

Veronica.

The sexy woman I had met at the kids' birthday party.

With the naughty smile.

And the MDMA.

They're both holding glasses of wine. They both look up as I walk in, and my wife grins at me drunkenly.

"You're home. Where have you *been?*"

For a few moments I forget how to talk. My wife smiles at me with shining lips.

I'm frozen on the spot, like an idiot. "What... what are you kids up to?"

Veronica flicks her hair and tilts her glass towards me.

"Seeing who can get the drunkest. Your wife is winning."

Claire nods, raising a finger.

"I am *quite* the talent."

They both cackle. Claire leans into Veronica and they press their heads together drunkenly. Veronica wraps her arms around Claire's shoulders, beaming at her.

For one heart-stopping moment, their noses circle each other, as though they're about to *kiss...*

... then Claire pulls away, clearing her throat suggestively. She takes her legs off Veronica's knees and the other woman stands up and smooths down her dress.

Claire smiles at me, all prim and proper.

"You remember Veronica? You met her at the

barbecue a few weeks back."

She walks over to where I'm standing and politely holds out a hand.

Veronica. With the naughty smile.

My lips are numb, my throat is dry, and when I speak it's with a rasp.

"Veronica?"

She raises an eyebrow and gives me that naughty smile.

"My friends call me Ronnie."

The world falls away from under my feet.

I ignore Veronica's extended hand.

Instead, I wrap a hand around her waist and before anyone can say anything I pull her close…

…and kiss her.

Chapter 99

Time slows down.

The naughty smile becomes a grin as our tongues touch.

I hear Claire gasp on the couch, but she doesn't stand up.

Ronnie opens her mouth, pressing her body against mine, inviting.

My hand slides around her hip to take a firm grasp on her pert ass.

She tastes like champagne and she tastes like my wife and I'm light-headed, kissing her hungrily.

She slips her knee between mine and our waists push together. She must be able to feel the hard bulge growing in my jeans because she leans into it.

And then abruptly she moves away. With a sparkle in her eye, she takes my hand and leads me back to the couch, where my wife is watching with a rapt expression.

We sit down, and Veronica turns that naughty smile towards my wife.

Mouth hanging open lustfully, eyes half-lidded, Claire reaches for her.

I watch their tongues darting together, watch Claire reach her hands into Ronnie's dark hair, watch their cheeks flush.

The kiss goes on.

When it finally breaks, they both look at me, their eyes bright.

I can feel the stupid grin spreading across my face but I can't do anything about it.

They giggle at my expression, then kiss again. Longer this time. Eyes closed.

Claire's hand wanders over Ronnie's shoulder, down to her breast. Their breathing is heavier now when the kiss ends.

Veronica bites her lip as Claire pulls away and turns towards me.

My wife kisses me hard, hungrily, passionately.

While my eyes are closed I feel Veronica's hands running up the top of my thighs.

Claire turns and kisses Ronnie, who's kneeling on the floor between my legs now, her hands playing softly over my jeans. They kiss, again, and then Claire pulls back and pushes Veronica towards me.

Ronnie's kiss is fresh with chardonnay, her

tongue small and soft and sensual.

My brain fuzzes over.

While I'm kissing Ronnie, I reach around Claire's hips and take hold of her magnificent ass. Claire sits up for long enough to take off her blouse before nuzzling into me, her breath hot on my neck.

Veroncia's body is pressing more urgently against mine, so I pull back and push Claire gently towards her. The girls kiss again, hungrily, while I run one hand over Claire's ass and the other over Ronnie's hips.

Without opening her eyes, Ronnie takes my hand and puts it on her breast.

I graze her nipple with my thumb and her whole body jerks. She grasps at Claire, kissing her, moaning a little.

I gently undo the buttons of Veronica's blouse and wisp it away.

Their skin feels incredible under my hands. Claire turns to kiss me again and I use my Fonzy move to unlatch her bra. Ronnie pulls it out of the way and takes Claire's nipple between her lips.

Claire gasps into my mouth then turns Ronnie's face up for another deep kiss.

The three of us take turns kissing softly. I run my hand around Ronnie's black bra and with a flick of my wrist it is gone.

"Wow. One hand." Veronica giggles, her voice rough.

"He thinks he's pretty smooth." Claire grins.

Her hand is running over the bulge in my jeans.

"He's definitely pretty hard."

She reaches out and takes Ronnie's hand, guides it to my zipper.

"See?"

Veronica squeezes my hardness and I take her sweet little nipple between my lips.

They kiss again, then Claire's hands work away at my belt and my zipper before Ronnie pulls my jeans off and away.

I hold Claire against my chest and kiss her deeply as Veronica's hands tickle up my bare thighs.

My wife reaches down and pulls my underwear away.

My cock is suddenly wrapped in her friend's waiting hands.

I can't help but groan.

Claire shifts away from me, settles onto the floor next to Veroncia. They kiss again, their hands running over my balls, wrapping around my shaft.

They look fucking *amazing*.

I gently push their bodies together so that their nipples meet – Claire's are slightly larger and darker than Ronnie's light pink buttons.

They both glance down at their touching nipples and smile, pushing against each other, their hands moving faster and more urgently, their kisses hungrier, their cheeks high with colour, their eyes sparkling with excitement.

Veronica wraps her hand around my knob, twisting gently, and I reach down and take a handful of her ass. She leans in to kiss me, her tongue dancing around mine, while Claire lowers her face down to my cock.

Her tongue presses into my shaft and she slowly licks her way up to the head. Ronnie watches her take me into her mouth. I squeeze Ronnie's ass and she wraps Claire's hair around her hand. Claire lifts her head as she runs her lips up the side of my shaft, looking into Veronica's eyes all the while.

Smiling, Ronnie leans down to face her.

Her tongue flicks the other side of my shaft.

Oh sweet *Jesus.*

Their warm tongues glide over me, tickling and firm. They kiss around the head of my cock and Claire's hand reaches down into Ronnie's lap.

While Ronnie takes me properly into her mouth, Claire peels off her friend's tights and then her own.

Both naked now except for their panties, they take turns sucking and licking me, their hands running over each other, encouraging, fascinated.

Claire buckles a little as Veronica reaches into her panties and she bears down on me, taking almost all of my length into her throat. I can't stifle a loud groan.

While my wife sucks me, I pull her friend up for a kiss, sneaking my hand into her panties, reaching for her soft, warm mound. She pushes against my fingers, looking into my eyes, kissing me while Claire works my cock with her mouth.

Abruptly Claire is standing, pulling me to my feet. I take Ronnie's hand.

The three of us walk to the bedroom together.

I'm not sure if my feet are even touching the floor.

Chapter 100

None of us speak.

Claire climbs onto the bed and pushes me onto my back. Holding my shoulders down, she turns around and puts her knees either side of my head, lowering her pussy onto my face.

It looks wonderful, delicious, and I can't help but growl hungrily as I glide my tongue over her lips.

I can feel her hand wrapping around the base of my cock and Ronnie's tongue circling the head. With another moan, I slip my tongue inside my wife.

Claire takes me into her mouth, while Ronnie gently licks at my balls. Claire's pussy tastes amazing. I can't work my tongue hard enough and I push her down onto my face to try and get it in deeper.

Claire suddenly sits bolt upright.

I hear it too – the patter of small feet on the

hallway floorboards.

With my wife's sweet pussy now hovering above my face, I look down to see her friend's lips wrapped around my dick.

Veronica doesn't take my cock out of her mouth. When I wrap my hand in her hair to make sure she doesn't, she looks up and notices me watching.

She gives me a slow wink and pulls me further down her throat. I hold her head, gently but firmly, and slowly fuck her mouth.

Claire climbs off the bed and quickly wraps a dressing gown around her naked form. She looks over her shoulder momentarily as she opens our bedroom door and slips through it.

I hear her pick up Little K just outside our bedroom door and carry her back up the hallway, her soothing voice hiding a touch of impatience.

For a moment, Ronnie and I are alone.

Veronica sits up and looks around, dishevelled.

"Where did she go?"

"One of the kids got up. She'll be back, don't worry."

She flashes that naughty smile again.

"I'm not worried."

She climbs up onto the bed and kneels next to me. Her arms curl around my neck and she pulls me close enough to kiss.

"Just surprised that I've got you to myself."

We kiss, long and hard. She's an amazing, hungry kisser. Without breaking the kiss, I pull her onto my lap, spreading her wide.

Her light, neat fuzz of pubic hair tickles my waist. My cock is still wet from her mouth, but it gets wetter as she teases it with her pussy lips.

I run my hands over her breasts, down to her hips. Her body is slender, fit, her skin salty and damp with sweat.

Her cheeks are flushed, her breath coming faster and faster.

"Fuck me," she whispers urgently into my ear. "Fuck me now!"

I lower my hips into the mattress and the head of my cock rests against her wetness. I'm so fucking hard it feels like my cock is made of steel.

Ronnie gasps as she pushes against me… then I'm inside her, squeezing my hardness into her tight cunt.

Her incredible, wet snugness makes my toes curl.

She wraps her arms around my head, pulling my face into her breasts as she takes me in deeper and deeper.

When I'm all the way in, she leans back, giving my hands free reign over her lithe nakedness. I watch my cock sliding in and out of her, getting wetter with every thrust.

With my hands holding the tops of her pale thighs, I grind her slowly.

She's watching me watching her, biting her lip, moving her hips in a slow circle.

Gazing back into her eyes, I slowly lick my thumb and then run it over her exposed clit. She groans, rocking her head back, bearing down on me.

Something makes me look up; my wife is standing just inside our bedroom door, watching me fuck her friend.

Chapter 101

There's no jealousy on Claire's face; her expression is an odd mingling of lust and… pride?

After a moment, she comes over to the bed, kneels next to us, reaches up and brushes Veronica's hair off her shoulder. She leans in to kiss her neck, but Veronica pulls her face up and kisses her properly, lustily.

Claire cups one of Ronnie's pert breasts, grazing her nipple with her thumb and Ronnie groans, thrusting faster, gasping for breath. Her cheeks are sexily flushed, her lips pink and shining.

One of my hands is on Ronnie's hip squeezing it as she fucks me, while the other sneaks up the inside of Claire's damp thigh.

Claire's pussy is soft and warm and she opens her legs a little so that I can slip two fingers inside her.

Suddenly Claire is gasping as well.

The two gorgeous women clutch at each other, kissing desperately, their breasts pushing together.

It kills my brain, watching them kiss, and I push Veronica down onto my cock, trying to get it further in. She feels fucking amazing.

"Oh fuck," she cries, her body stiffening.

I rock her back and forth, working against her arching back, my fingers plunging in and out of my wife with the same rhythm.

"Fuck her," Claire moans. "Give her that fucking cock!"

Claire reaches a gentle hand down, squeezes my shaft to Veronica's clit.

Ronnie bucks away at me, biting her lip, trying to keep her voice down. Claire takes a firm grip on the base of my cock and slowly stirs it around in her friend's pussy.

Ronnie cries out, her hips bucking, her thighs shaking uncontrollably.

"Oh... my *fucking... god!*"

Veronica collapses on top of me, her body melting into a warm entanglement of skin and sweat.

Claire withdraws her hand as Ronnie takes a gasping, laughing breath.

"Oh shit. I just came *so hard.*"

Grinning, Claire kisses Veronica while I slowly slide in and out of her. I'm still so stiff.

I gently toy with her pussy, exploring her soft warmth with my hard flesh.   Veronica gasps, shivering again, then giggles and kisses me lightly.

"Somebody wants more, I think."

She detangles herself, climbs off.

I do want more.

I reach for my wife.

Chapter 102

"Wait," murmurs Claire.

Instead of climbing onto my lap, she pushes Ronnie down on to the mattress next to me and climbs on top of her, kissing her, waving her perfectly curved derrière in the air.

I love seeing their bodies moving together and I run my fingers up Claire's spine as she wriggles down between Ronnie's thighs.

On Claire's first lick, Veronica whimpers. On the second, she grabs my neck in a tight grip and by the third she is pushing her tongue against mine. Her body moves in waves. Her hand finds my hardness again and she squeezes me as she moans.

It feels so fucking good, especially when Claire leans over to briefly take my cock in her mouth, sucking Ronnie's juices off my stiff shaft, before returning her attention to her friend's freshly fucked pussy.

After a couple of minutes, I can't take anymore,

so I get up to kneel behind my wife.

Claire's eyes are closed, her lips pushed against Veronica's, her tongue darting this way and that. When I push my cock against her, my hands tight on her hips, she wriggles her knees apart another inch so that I can ease inside.

She's so wet that I slide in deeply and she cries out, pushing back against me. I push it all the way in hard and hold her there, the way she likes it, so that she can grind against it.

Her hands clutch at Ronnie's waist. Her tongue works faster.

Long, slow thrusts, rocking against Claire's gorgeous ass, watching her push her fingers and tongue into her friend's pussy, watching Ronnie squeezing at her own breasts and watching me fuck my wife...

This is what I wanted all along.

I slam into Claire, I hold her hips and fuck her for all I'm worth, her muffled cries getting louder with each thrust. Her pussy squeezes my cock deliciously, while her face pushes into Veronica's pussy.

Claire rocks between us, making guttural sounds of hunger that I've never heard before, her body stiffening around me...

Ronnie's moaning is getting high-pitched again – Claire's fingers are moving faster and faster as I fuck her faster and faster...

With her hands squeezing the pillows behind her head and her hips lifting off the mattress, Ronnie cries out again, shuddering, swearing.

Claire shakes once, twice, squealing... then slows down all at once, her body supple.

I slow down too.

Ronnie settles back, breathing hard, and she laughs a little disbelievingly.

Claire collapses on top of her and they both gasp, their breath mingling, their lovely faces beading with sweat.

But I'm not down with my wife yet.

I put my hands under her chest and pull her back up. At the same time, I sit back on my heels, so that I'm kneeling on the bed and she's sitting on my lap.

With a mind-numbing whine, my wife rotates her hips, pulling my cock with her tight pussy, then starts slowly pushing back onto me.

My hands are free to roam her delicious skin, to cup her sexy pointed tits, to tickle at her clit.

My cock is so fucking hard, and my wife is so fucking soft, and I plunge in and out of her.

As I'm stroking her pussy, my fingertips brushing my hard meat as it slides in and out of her, another hand tangles with mine.

Ronnie is kneeling in front of Claire now, kissing her, running her hands over my wife's bouncing body.

I feel her light fingers wrap around my shaft and it makes me gasp; when she reaches down and cups my balls, it makes me groan.

Veronica grins and disappears from view, while I wrap my arms around Claire's shoulders and force her body down onto my cock.

Abruptly my entire body tingles as a warm tongue slide over the skin of my balls.

I've never felt something so fucking *amazing*. My mind is blank, white, my whole universe wrapped in the tight grip of my wife's cunt, on the tip of her friend's warm tongue.

I stop moving as the tongue explores upwards, along the base of my shaft, just below Claire's tight, quivering lips.

Claire cries out a moment later as Ronnie's delightful tongue reaches her. The tongue presses into my cock again momentarily, its rough softness teasing my stiffness, then it's gone again.

Claire rocks against me gently, squeezes me deep inside.

My body melts as Ronnie's tongue slides back and forth between my hardness and Claire's softness and back again.

It's too much.

It's *everything*.

I gently sink my teeth into Claire's shoulder and breathe into her ear.

"Oh *fuck*. You're fucking *amazing*."

She whimpers and bears down on my cock another couple of times for good measure and then she's abruptly moving away.

My body is tingling as my throbbing flesh waves in the air for a moment… before Ronnie takes it deep into her mouth.

She greedily sucks Claire's juices off my throbbing cock and then Claire is there too, laying half on top of her. Their hands squeeze me, excruciatingly hard and slow, their mouths take turns licking and sucking and drawing me deeper and…

And I'm cumming.

Cumming harder than I knew it was possible to cum, coming as if it's the first time, cumming so hard that my vision blurs and my ears ring and my body fills with excruciating, pleasure.

My body shakes.

My head is weightless.

The world turns white.

I feel movement through my body, a flood of pressure release, a flow of power, an explosion of life force.

They squeeze my balls, their tongues teasing my stiff, spasming cock, their pink lips dripping my cum onto their delicate fingertips.

My body shudders again, ultra-sensitive to their touching.

They play with me, fascinated, taking turns to suck out every last drop until their eyes meet and they grin and pull each other close for a messy, sticky kiss.

It's the most gorgeous fucking thing that I've ever seen.

As soon as my head stops spinning, I bend down to kiss them both gently.

"Joe," Veronica whispers in a serious voice.

Claire bites her lip, suddenly apprehensive.

Ronnie clears her throat and tries again.

"Joe… there is cum *everywhere,* oh my fucking god…"

Claire snorts laughter, and I do too.

Chapter 103

A little while later we climb out of bed. Claire pulls on one of my t-shirts and lends Ronnie her night gown.

Even though I came – and came *hard* - only a few minutes earlier, I find their bare legs captivating. I want to weave myself between them again, to be wrapped up in them.

"Maybe…" Claire catches my eye. "We could use something to pep us up a bit?"

I couldn't agree more.

Ronnie's eyes are shining.

There's enough cocaine for a couple of lines each.

There's enough weed for a joint each, though Claire and RONNIE opt to share one.

We sit on the deck, beneath the autumn sky. By the time we finish snorting and smoking and drinking, my blood is fizzing, my head is empty.

I can feel the shine of every individual star on

my skin.

The slightest stirring of breeze feels like a kiss from the universe.

The women chat about something, their voices low and excited. I'm listening but I'm a million miles away as well, the coke barrelling through my veins and filling the sky with wonder.

Their skin catches the moonlight. Their bare legs make my blood pound.

I need to press my face against those thighs.

"Come on."

I stand up and hold out a hand to each of them.

They look at each other and snort laughter – but they come.

Hand in hand in hand, we go inside together, back to the bedroom.

We don't come out for a long time.

Chapter 104

C laire and I can't look at each other without
giggling.

It feels like we're teenagers again.

What an incredible night.

I am no longer a man who has never had a
threesome. It turns out that Claire had planned
the whole thing. She told Veronica about the coke
and mentioned that I might be willing to share
it… if they convinced me together.

She thought that we would have the powder
and some champagne, then see what happened…
maybe one thing would lead to another.

I didn't even get any champagne. Claire loves
teasing me about that. Stopping for a few lines
later on meant that the three of us were still
wrapped around each other as the sun came up.

It was a night I'll never forget, for all the right
reasons.

When Veronica left, she gave each of us a warm

kiss and a broad grin.

The next day, I told Claire about reading her messages with Ronnie, about how I knew she was cheating on me. I told her how it almost broke me.

I told her how unworthy I had felt, how desperate I was to save my self-esteem, how losing our relationship had felt like the end of the world.

I admitted what happened with Lisa, with SecretChloe, and the girl from Faux Mo.

She cried and she struggled with it - but she forgave me pretty quickly. She held me and made me promise never to play around again... unless she's there to join in.

It really is ridiculous how much different the world suddenly seems. Now it feels like I actually belong here. I feel wanted. Desired. Seen. I feel like a million bucks.

I deleted X from my phone. In fact, every trace of the past few months is gone... except for this document you hold in your hands.

I've spent so many hours hunched over my phone - on buses, in meetings, in bed - writing all of this down more or less as it happened.

For a while I thought it might end up being my suicide note, or a grim record of my marriage dissolving.

But Claire insisted that I keep it. She's read it

several times already. She cries, she laughs, and then she devours me.

My wife and I are closer than ever.

She looks at me the way she used to, when we were young.

We can't keep our hands off each other.

I look and feel better than I ever have.

I've got a new swagger.

And a new camera. I don't know where Claire and I will go from here… but I can't wait to find out.

About the Author

Joey D'Angelo's stories are part memoir and part fiction, a mix of gritty realism, human drama and explicit erotica. He sees writing as a therapeutic way to shed light on the parts of his life that would be otherwise left in the dark.

Joey was born in Sydney but has lived in Tasmania, Australia, for most of his life.

You can connect with me on:

🐦 https://x.com/theuglyhusband

www.ingramcontent.com/pod-product-compliance
Lightning Source LLC
Chambersburg PA
CBHW070242140726
47909CB00019B/2039